A Kentucky Cardinal

James Lane Allen

Contents

A Kentucky Cardinal

BY

James Lane Allen

A KENTUCKY CARDINAL

I

ALL this New-year's Day of 1850 the sun shone cloudless but wrought no thaw. Even the landscapes of frost on the window-panes did not melt a flower, and the little trees still keep their silvery boughs arched high above the jewelled avenues. During the afternoon a lean hare limped twice across the lawn, and there was not a creature stirring to chase it. Now the night is bitter cold, with no sounds outside but the cracking of the porches as they freeze tighter. Even the north wind seems grown too numb to move. I had determined to convert its coarse, big noise into something sweet—as may often be done by a little art with the things of this life—and so stretched a horse-hair above the opening between the window sashes; but the soul of my harp has departed. I hear but the comfortable roar and snap of hickory logs, at long intervals a deeper breath from the dog stretched on his side at my feet, and the crickets under the hearth-stones. They have to thank me for that nook. One chill afternoon I came upon a whole company of them on the western slope of a woodland mound, so lethargic that I thumped them repeatedly before they could so much as get their senses. There was a branch near by, and the smell of mint in the air, so that had they been young Ken-tuckians one might have had a clew to the situation. With an ear for winter minstrelsy, I brought two home in a handkerchief, and assigned them an elegant suite of apartments under a loose brick.

But the finest music in the room is that which streams out to the ear of the spirit in many an exquisite strain from the hanging shelf of books on the opposite wall. Every volume there is an instrument which some melodist of the mind created and set vibrating with music, as a flower shakes out its perfume or a star shakes out its light. Only listen, and they soothe all care, as though the silken-soft leaves of poppies had been made vocal and poured into the ear.

Towards dark, having seen to the comfort of a household of kind, faithful fellow-beings, whom man in his vanity calls the lower animals, I went last to walk under the cedars in the front yard, listening to that music which is at once so cheery and so sad—the low chirping of birds at dark winter twilights as they gather in from the frozen fields, from snow-buried shrubbery and hedge-rows, and settle down for the night in the depths of the evergreens, the only refuge from their enemies and shelter from the blast. But this evening they made no ado about their home-coming. To-day perhaps none had ventured forth. I am most uneasy when the red-bird is forced by hunger to leave the covert of his cedars, since he, on the naked or white landscapes of winter, offers the most far-shining and beautiful mark for Death. I stepped across to the tree in which a pair of these birds roost and shook it, to make sure they were at home, and felt relieved when they fluttered into the next with the quick startled notes they utter when aroused.

The longer I live here, the better satisfied I am in having pitched my earthly camp-fire, gypsylike, on the edge of a town, keeping it on one side, and the green fields, lanes, and woods on the other. Each, in turn, is to me as a magnet to the needle. At times the needle of my nature points towards the country. On that side everything is poetry. I wander over field and forest, and through me runs a glad current of feeling that is like a clear brook across the meadows of May. At others the needle veers round, and I go to town—to the massed haunts of the highest animal and cannibal. That way nearly everything is prose. I can feel the prose rising in me as I step along, like hair on the back of a dog, long before any other dogs are in sight. And, indeed, the case is much that of a country dog come to town, so that growls are in order at every corner. The only being in the universe at which I have ever snarled, or with which I have rolled over in the mud and fought like a common cur, is Man.

Among my neighbors who furnish me much of the plain prose of life, the nearest hitherto has been a bachelor named Jacob Mariner. I called him my rain-crow, because the sound of his voice awoke apprehensions of falling weather. A visit from him was an endless drizzle. For Jacob came over to expound his minute symptoms;

and had everything that he gave out on the subject of human ailments been written down, it must have made a volume as large, as solemn, and as inconvenient as a family Bible. My other nearest neighbor lives across the road—a widow, Mrs. Walters. I call Mrs. Walters my mocking-bird, because she reproduces by what is truly a divine arrangement of the throat the voices of the town. When she flutters across to the yellow settee under the grape-vine and balances herself lightly with expectation, I have but to request that she favor me with a little singing, and soon the air is vocal with every note of the village songsters. After this, Mrs. Walters usually begins to flutter in a motherly way around the subject of my symptoms.

Naturally it has been my wish to bring about between this rain-crow and mockingbird the desire to pair with one another. For, if a man always wanted to tell his symptoms and a woman always wished to hear about them, surely a marriage compact on the basis of such a passion ought to open up for them a union of overflowing and indestructible felicity. They should associate as perfectly as the compensating metals of a pendulum, of which the one contracts as the other expands. And then I should be a little happier myself. But the perversity of life! Jacob would never confide in Mrs. Walters. Mrs. Walters would never inquire for Jacob.

Now poor Jacob is dead, of no complaint apparently, and with so few symptoms that even the doctors did not know what was the matter, and the upshot of this talk is that his place has been sold, and I am to have new neighbors. What a disturbance to a man living on the edge of a quiet town!

Tidings of the calamity came to-day from Mrs. Walters, who flew over and sang—sang even on a January afternoon—in a manner to rival her most vociferous vernal execution. But the poor creature was so truly distressed that I followed her to the front gate, and we twittered kindly at each other over the fence, and ruffled our plumage with common disapproval. It is marvellous how a member of her sex will conceive dislike of people that she has never seen ; but birds are sensible of heat or cold long before either arrives, and it may be that this mocking-bird feels something wrong at the quill end of her feathers.

II

MRS. WALTERS this morning with more news touching our incoming neighbors. Whenever I have faced towards this aggregation of unwelcome individuals, I have beheld it moving towards me as a thick gray mist, shutting out nature beyond. Perhaps they are approaching this part of the earth like a comet that carries its tail before it, and I am already enveloped in a disturbing, befogging nebulosity.

There is still no getting the truth, but it appears that they are a family of consequence in their way—which, of course, may be a very poor way. Mrs. Margaret Cobb, mother, lately bereaved of her husband, Joseph Cobb, who fell among the Kentucky boys at the battle of Buena' Vista. A son, Joseph Cobb, now cadet at West Point, with a desire to die like his father, but destined to die—who knows?—in a war that may break out in this country about the negroes. Then there is a daughter, Miss Georgiana Cobb, who embroiders blue-and-pink-worsted dogs on black foot-cushions, makes far-off crayon trees that look like sheep in the act of variously getting up and lying down on a hillside, and, when the dew is falling and the moon is the shape of the human lips, touches her guitar with maidenly solicitude. Lastly, a younger daughter, who is in the half-fledged state of becoming educated.

While not reconciled, I am resigned. The young man when at home may wish to practise the deadly vocation of an American soldier of the period over the garden fence at my birds, in which case he and I could readily fight a duel, and help maintain an honored custom of the commonwealth. The older daughter will sooner or later turn loose on my heels one of her pack of blue dogs. If this should befall me in the spring, and I survive the dog, I could retort with a dish of strawberries and a copy of "Lalla Rookh"; if in the fall, with a basket of grapes and Thomson's "Seasons," after which there would be no further exchange of hostilities. The younger daughter, being a school-girl, will occasionally have to be subdued with green apples and salt. The mother could easily give trouble; or she might be one of those few women to know whom is to know the best that there is in all this faulty world.

The middle of February. The depths of winter reached. Thoughtful, thoughtless words—the depths of winter. Everything gone inward and downward from surface and summit, Nature at low tide. In its time will come the height of summer, when the tides of life will rise to the tree-tops, or be dashed as silvery insect spray all but to the clouds. So bleak a season touches my concern for birds, which never seem quite at home in this world; and the winter has been most lean and hungry for them. Many snows have fallen—snows that are as raw cotton spread over their breakfast-table, and cutting off connection between them and its bounties. Next summer I must let the weeds grow up in my garden, so that they may have a better chance for seeds above the stingy level of the universal white. Of late I have opened a pawnbroker's shop for my hard-pressed brethren in feathers, lending at a fearful rate of interest; for every borrowing Lazarus will have to pay me back in due time by monthly instalments of singing. I shall have mine own again with usury. But were a man never so usurious, would he not lend a winter seed for a summer song? Would he refuse to invest his stale crumbs in an orchestra of divine instruments and a choir of heavenly voices? And to-day, also, I ordered from a nursery-man more trees of holly, juniper, and fir, since the storm-beaten cedars will have to come down. For in Kentucky, when the forest is naked, and every shrub and hedge-row bare, what would become of our birds in the universal rigor and exposure of the world if there were no evergreens—nature's hostelries for the homeless ones? Living in the depths of these, they can keep snow, ice, and wind at bay; prying eyes cannot watch them, nor enemies so well draw near; cones or seed or berries are their store; and in those untrodden chambers each can have the sacred company of his mate. But wintering here has terrible risks which few run. Scarcely in autumn have the leaves begun to drop from their high perches silently downward when the birds begin to drop away from the bare boughs silently southward. Lo! some morning the leaves are on the ground, and the birds have vanished. The species that remain, or that come to us then, wear the hues of the season, and melt into the tone of Nature's background—blues, grays, browns, with touches of white on tail and breast and wing for coming flecks of snow.

Save only him—proud, solitary stranger in our unfriendly land—the fiery gros-beak. Nature in Kentucky has no wintry harmonies for him. He could find these only among the tufts of the October sumac, or in the gum-tree when it stands a pillar of red twilight fire in the dark November woods, or in the far depths of the crimson sunset skies, where, indeed, he seems to have been nested, and whence to have come as a messenger of beauty, bearing on his wings the light of his diviner home.

With almost everything earthly that he touches this high herald of the trees is in contrast. Among his kind he is without a peer. Even when the whole company of summer voyagers have sailed back to Kentucky, singing and laughing and kissing one another under the enormous green umbrella of Nature's leaves, he still is beyond them all in loveliness. But when they have been wafted away again to brighter skies and to soft islands over the sea, and he is left alone on the edge of that Northern world which he has dared invade and inhabit, it is then, amid black clouds and drifting snows, that the gorgeous cardinal stands forth in the ideal picture of his destiny. For it is then that his beauty is most conspicuous, and that Death, lover of the peerless, strikes at him from afar. So that he retires to the twilight solitude of his wild fortress. Let him even show his noble head and breast at a slit in its green window-shades, and a ray flashes from it to the eye of a cat; let him, as spring comes on, burst out in desperation and mount to the tree-tops which he loves, and his gleaming red coat betrays him to the poised hawk as to a distant sharpshooter; in the barn near by an owl is waiting to do his night marketing at various tender-meat stalls; and, above all, the eye and heart of man are his diurnal and nocturnal foe. What wonder if he is so shy, so rare, so secluded, this flame-colored prisoner in dark-green chambers, who has only to be seen or heard and Death adjusts an arrow.

No vast Southern swamps or forest of pine here into which he may plunge. If he shuns man in Kentucky, he must haunt the long lonely river valleys where the wild cedars grow. If he comes into this immediate swarming pastoral region, where the people, with ancestral love of privacy, and not from any kindly thought of him, plant evergreens around their country homes, he must live under the very guns and amid the pitfalls of the enemy. Surely, could the first male of the species have foreseen how, through the generations of his race to come, both their beauty and their song, which were meant to announce them to Love, would also announce them to Death, he must have blanched snow-white with despair and turned as mute as a stone. Is it this flight from the inescapable just behind that makes the singing of the red-bird thoughtful and plaintive, and, indeed, nearly all the wild sounds of nature so like the outcry of the doomed? He will sit for a long time silent and motionless in the heart of a cedar, as if absorbed in the tragic memories of his race. Then, softly, wearily, he will call out to you and to the whole world: Peace . . Peace . . Peace . . Peace . . Peace . .!—the most melodious sigh that ever issued from the clefts of a dungeon.

For color and form, brilliant singing, his very enemies, and the bold nature he has never lost, I have long been most interested in this bird. Every year several pairs make their appearance about my place. This winter especially I have been feeding a pair; and there should be finer music in the spring, and a lustier brood in summer.

III

MARCH has gone like its winds. The other night as I lay awake with that yearning which often beats within, there fell from the upper air the notes of the wild gander as he wedged his way onward by faith, not by sight, towards his distant bourn. I rose and, throwing open the shutters, strained eyes towards the unseen and unseeing explorer, startled, as a half-asleep soldier might be startled by the faint bugle-call of his commander, blown to him from the clouds. What far-off lands, streaked with mortal dawn, does he believe in? In what soft sylvan waters will he bury his tired breast? Always when I hear his voice, often when not, I too desire to be up and gone out of these earthly marshes where hunts the dark Fowler—gone to some vast, pure, open sea, where, one by one, my scattered kind, those whom I love and those who love me, will arrive in safety, there to be together.

March is a month when the needle of my nature dips towards the country. I am away, greeting everything as it wakes out of winter sleep, stretches arms upward and legs downward, and drinks goblet after goblet of young sunshine. I must find the dark green snowdrop, and sometimes help to remove from her head, as she lifts it slowly from her couch, the frosted nightcap, which the old Nurse would still insist that she should wear. The pale green tips of daffodils are a thing of beauty. There is the sun-struck brook of the field, underneath the thin ice of which drops form and fall, form and fall, like big round silvery eyes that grow bigger and brighter with astonishment that you should laugh at them as they vanish. But most I love to see Nature do her spring house-cleaning in Kentucky, with the rain-clouds for her water-buckets and the winds for her brooms. What an amount of drenching and sweeping she can do in a day! How she dashes pailful and pailful into every corner, till the whole earth is as clean as a new floor! Another day she attacks the piles of dead leaves, where they have lain since last October, and scatters them in a trice, so that every cranny may be sunned and aired. Or, grasping her long brooms by the handles, she will go into the woods and beat the icicles off the big trees as a housewife would brush down cobwebs; so that the released limbs straighten up like a man who has gotten out of debt, and almost say to you, joyfully, "Now, then, we are all right again!" This done, she begins to hang up soft new curtains at the forest windows, and to spread over her floor a new carpet of an emerald loveliness such as no mortal looms could ever have woven. And then, at last, she sends out invitations through the South, and even to some tropical lands, for the birds to come and spend the summer in Kentucky. The invitations are sent out in March, and accepted in April and May, and by June her house is full of visitors.

Not the eyes alone love Nature in March. Every other sense hies abroad. My tongue hunts for the last morsel of wet snow on the northern root of some aged oak. As one goes early to a concert-hall with a passion even for the preliminary tuning of the musicians, so my ear sits alone in the vast amphitheatre of Nature and waits for the earliest warble of the blue-bird, which seems to start up somewhere behind the heavenly curtains. And the scent of spring, is it not the first lyric of the nose—that despised poet of the senses?

But this year I have hardly glanced at the small choice edition of Nature's spring verses. This by reason of the on-coming Cobbs, at the mere mention of whom I feel as though I were plunged up to my eyes in a vat of the prosaic. Some days ago work-men went into the house and all but scoured the very memory of Jacob off the face of the earth. Then there has been need to quiet Mrs. Walters.

Mrs. Walters does not get into our best society; so that the town is to her like a pond to a crane: she wades round it, going in as far as she can, and snatches up such small fry as come shoreward from the middle. In this way lately I have gotten hints of what is stirring in the vasty deeps of village opinion.

Mrs. Cobb is charged, among other dreadful things, with having ordered of the town manufacturer a carriage that is to be as fine as President Taylor's, and with marching into church preceded by a servant, who bears her prayer-book on a velvet cushion. What if she rode in Cinderella's coach, or had her prayer-book carried before her on the back of a Green River turtle? But to her sex she promises to be an invidious Christian. I am rather disturbed by the gossip regarding the elder daughter. But this is so conflicting that one impression is made only to be effaced by another.

A week ago their agent wanted to buy my place. I was so outraged that I got down my map of Kentucky to see where these peculiar beings originate. They come from a little town in the northwestern corner of the State, on the Ohio River, named Henderson— named from that Richard Henderson who in the year 1775 bought about half of Kentucky from the Cherokees, and afterwards, as president of his purchase, addressed the first legislative assembly ever held in the West, seated under a big elm-tree outside the walls of Boonsborough fort. These people must be his heirs, or they would never have tried to purchase my few Sabine acres. It is no surprise to discover that they are from the Green River country. They must bathe often in that stream. I suppose they wanted my front yard to sow it in pennyroyal, the characteristic growth of those districts. They surely distil it and use it as a perfume on their handkerchiefs. It was perhaps from the founder of this family that Thomas Jefferson got authority for his statement that the Ohio is the most beautiful river in the world—unless, indeed, the President formed that notion of the Ohio upon lifting his eyes to it from the contemplation of Green River. Henderson! Green River region! To this town and to the blue-grass country as Boeotia to Attica in the days of Pericles. Hereafter I shall call these people my Green River Boeotians.

A few days later their agent again, a little frigid, very urgent—this time to buy me out on my own terms, any terms. But what was back of all this, I inquired. I did not know these people, had never done them a favor. Why, then, such determination to have me removed? Why such bitterness, vindictiveness, ungovernable passion?

That was the point, he replied. This family had never wronged me, I had never even seen them. Yet they had heard of nothing but my intense dislike of them and opposition to their becoming my neighbors. They could not forego their plans, but they were quite willing to give me the chance of leaving their vicinity, on whatever I might regard the most advantageous terms.

Oh, my mocking-bird, my mocking-bird! When you have been sitting on other front porches, have you, by the divine law of your being, been reproducing your notes as though they were mine, and even pouring forth the little twitter that was meant for your private ear?

As March goes out, two things more and more I hear—the cardinal has begun to mount to the bare tops of the locust-trees and scatter his notes downward, and over the way the workmen whistle and sing. The bird is too shy to sit in any tree on that side of the yard. But his eye and ear are studying them curiously. Sometimes I even fancy that he sings to them with a plaintive sort of joy, as though he were saying, "Welcome—go away!"

IV

THE Cobbs will be the death of me before they get here. The report spread that they and I had already had a tremendous quarrel, and that, rather than live beside them, I had sold them my place. This set flowing towards me for days a stream of people, like a line of ants passing to and from the scene of a terrific false alarm. I had nothing to do but sit perfectly still and let each ant, as it ran up, touch me with its antennae, get the countersign, and turn back to the village ant-hill. Not all, however. Some remained to hear me abuse the Cobbs; or, counting on my support, fell to abusing the Cobbs themselves. When I made not a word of reply, except to assure them that I really had not quarreled with the Cobbs, had nothing against the Cobbs, and was immensely delighted that the Cobbs were coming, they went away amazingly cool and indignant. And for days I continued to hear such things attributed to me that, had that young West-Pointer been in the neighborhood, and known how to shoot, he must infallibly have blown my head off me, as any Kentucky gentleman would.

Others of my visitors, having heard that I was not to sell my place, were so glad of it that they walked around my garden and inquired for my health and the prospect for fruit. For the season has come when the highest animal begins to pay me some attention. During the winter, having little to contribute to the community, I drop from communal notice. But there are certain ladies who bow sweetly to me when my roses and honeysuckles burst into bloom; a fat old cavalier of the South begins to shake hands with me when my asparagus bed begins to send up its tender stalks; I am in high favor with two or three young ladies at the season of lilies and sweet-pea; there is one old soul who especially loves rhubarb pies, which she makes to look like little latticed porches in front of little green skies, and it is she who remembers me and my row of pie-plant; and still another, who knows better than cat-birds when currants are ripe. Above all, there is a preacher, who thinks my sins are as scarlet so long as my strawberries are, and plants himself in my bed at that time to reason with me of judgment to come; and a doctor, who gets despondent about my constitution in pear-time—after which my health seems to return, but never my pears.

So that, on the whole, from May till October I am the bright side of the moon, and the telescopes of the town are busy observing my phenomena; after which it is as though I had rolled over on my dark side, there to lie forgotten till once more the sun entered the proper side of the zodiac. But let me except always the few steadily luminous spirits I know, with whom is no variableness, neither shadow of turning. If any one wishes to become famous in a community, let him buy a small farm on the edge of it and cultivate fruits, berries, and flowers, which he freely gives away or lets be freely taken.

All this has taken freely of my swift April days. Besides, I have made me a new side-porch, made it myself, for I like to hammer and drive things home, and because the rose on the old one had rotted it from post to shingle. And then, when I had tacked the rose in place again, the little old window opening above it made that side of my house look like a boy in his Saturday hat and Sunday breeches. So in went a large new window; and now these changes have mysteriously offended Mrs, Walters, who says the town is laughing at me for trying to outdo the Cobbs, The highest animal is the only one who is divinely gifted with such noble discernment. But I am not sorry to have my place look its best. When they see it, they will perhaps understand why I was not to be driven out by a golden cracker on their family whip. They could not have bought my little woodland pasture, where for a generation has been picnic and muster and Fourth-of-July ground, and where the brave fellows met to volunteer for the Mexican war. They could not have bought even the heap of brush back of my wood-pile, where the brown thrashers build.

V

IN May I am of the earth earthy. The soul loses its wild white pinions; the heart puts forth its short, powerful wings, heavy with heat and color, that flutter, but do not lift it off the ground. The month comes and goes, and not once do I think of lifting my eyes to the stars. The very sunbeams fall on the body as a warm golden net, and keep thought and feeling from escape. Nature uses beauty now not to uplift, but to entice. I find her intent upon the one general business of seeing that no type of her creatures gets left out of the generations. Studied in my yard full of birds, as with a condensing-glass of the world, she can be seen enacting among them the dramas of history. Yesterday, in the secret recess of a walnut, I saw the beginning of the Trojan war. Last week I witnessed the battle of Actium fought out in mid-air. And down among my hedges— indeed, openly in my very barn-yard—there is a perfectly scandalous Salt Lake City.

And while I am watching the birds, they are watching me. Not a little fop among them, having proposed and been accepted, but perches on a limb, and has the air of putting his hands mannishly under his coat-tails and crying out at me, "Hello! Adam, what were you made for?" "You attend to your business, and I'll attend to mine," I answer. "You have one May; I have twenty-five!" He didn't wait to hear. He caught sight of a pair of clear brown eyes peeping at him out of a near tuft of leaves, and sprang thither with open arms and the sound of a kiss.

But if I have twenty-five Mays remaining, are not some Mays gone? Ah, well! Better a single May with the right mate than the full number with the wrong. And where is she—the right one? If she ever comes near my yard and answers my whistle, I'll know it; and then I'll teach these popinjays in blue coats and white pantaloons what Adam was made for.

But the wrong one—there's the terror! Only think of so composite a phenomenon as Mrs. Walters, for instance, adorned with limp nightcap and stiff curl-papers, like garnishes around a leg of roast mutton, waking up beside me at four o'clock in the morning as some gray-headed love-bird of Madagascar, and beginning to chirp and trill in an ecstasy!

The new neighbors have come—mother, younger daughter, and servants. The son is at West Point; and the other daughter lingers a few days, unable, no doubt, to tear herself away from her beloved pennyroyal and dearest Green River. They are quiet; have borrowed nothing from any one in the neighborhood; have well-dressed, well-trained servants; and one begins to be a little impressed. The curtains they have put up at the windows suggest that the whole nest is being lined with soft, cool, spotless loveliness, that is very restful and beguiling.

No one has called yet, since they are not at home till June; but Mrs. Walters has done some tall wading lately, and declares that people do not know what to think. They will know when the elder daughter arrives; for it is the worst member of the family that settles what the world shall think of the others.

If only she were not the worst! If only as I sat here beside my large new window, around which the old rose-bush has been trained and now is blooming, I could look across to her window where the white curtains hang, and feel that behind them sat, shy and gentle, the wood-pigeon for whom through Mays gone by I have been vaguely waiting!

And yet I do not believe that I could live a single year with only the sound of cooing in the house. A wood-pigeon would be the death of me.

VI

THIS morning, the 3d of June, the Undine from Green River rose above the waves.

The strawberry bed is almost under their windows. I had gone out to pick the first dish of the season for breakfast; for while I do not care to eat except to live, I never miss an opportunity of living upon strawberries.

I was stooping down and bending the wet leaves over, so as not to miss any, when a voice at the window above said, timidly and playfully,

"Are you the gardener?"

I picked on, turning as red as the berries. Then the voice said again,

"Old man, are you the gardener?"

Of course a person looking down carelessly on the stooping figure of any man, and seeing nothing but a faded straw hat, and arms and feet and ankles bent to-gether, might easily think him decrepit with age. Some things touch off my temper. But I answered, humbly,

"I am the gardener, madam."

"How much do you ask for your strawberries?"

"The gentleman who owns this place does not sell his strawberries. He gives them away, if he likes people. How much do you ask for your strawberries?"

"What a nice old gentleman! Is he having those picked to give away?"

"He is having these picked for his breakfast."

"Don't you think he'd like you to give me those, and pick him some more?"*

"I fear not, madam."

"Nevertheless, you might. He'd never know."

"I think he'd find it out."

"You are not afraid of him, are you?"

"I am when he gets mad."

"Does he treat you badly?"

"If he does, I always forgive him."

"He doesn't seem to provide you with very many clothes."

I picked on.

"But you seem nicely fed."

I picked on.

"What is his name, old man? Don't you like to talk?"

"Adam Moss."

"Such a green, cool, soft name! It is like his house and yard and garden. What does he do?"

"Whatever he pleases."

"You must not be impertinent to me, or I'll tell him. What does he like?"

"Birds—red-birds. What do you like?"

"Red-birds! How does he catch them? Throw salt on their tails?"

"He is a lover of Nature, madam, and particularly of birds."

"What does he know about birds? Doesn't he care for people?"

"He doesn't think many worth caring for."

"Indeed! And he is perfect, then, is he?"

"He thinks he is nearly as bad as any ; but that doesn't make the rest any better."

"Poor old gentleman! He must have the blues dreadfully. What does he do with his birds? Eat his robins, and stuff his cats, and sell his red-birds in cages?"

"He considers it part of his mission in life to keep them from being eaten or stuffed or caged."

"And you say he is nearly a hundred?"

He is something over thirty years of age, madam."

"Thirty? Surely we heard he was very old. Thirty! And does he live in that beautiful little old house all by himself?"

"I live with him!"

"You! Ha! ha! ha! And what is your name, you dear good old man?"

"Adam."

"Two Adams living in the same house! Are you the old Adam? I have heard so much of him."

At this I rose, pushed back my hat, and looked up at her.

"I am Adam Moss," I said, with distant politeness. "You can have these strawberries for your breakfast if you want them."

There was a low quick "Oh!" and she was gone, and the curtains closed over her face. It was rude; but neither ought she to have called me the old Adam. I have been thinking of one thing: why should she speak slightingly of my knowledge of birds? What does she know about them? I should like to inquire.

Late this afternoon I dressed up in my high gray wool hat, my fine long-tailed blue cloth coat with brass buttons, my pink waistcoat, frilled shirt, white cravat, and yellow nankeen trousers, and walked slowly several times around my strawberry bed. Did not see any more ripe strawberries.

Within the last ten days I have called twice upon the Cobbs, urged no doubt by an extravagant readiness to find them all that I feared they were not. How exquisite in life is the art of not seeing many things, and of forgetting many that have been seen! They received me as though nothing unpleasant had happened. Nor did the elder daughter betray that we had met. She has not forgotten, for more than once I surprised a light in her eyes as though she were laughing. She has not, it is certain, told even her mother and sister. Somehow this fact invests her character with a charm as of subterranean roominess and secrecy. Women who tell everything are like finger-bowls of clear water.

But it is Sylvia that pleases me. She must be about seventeen ; and so demure and confiding that I was ready to take her by the hand, lead her to the garden-gate, and say: Dear child, everything in here—butterflies, flowers, fruit, honey, everything—is yours ; come and go and gather as you like.

Yesterday morning I sent them a large dish of strawberries, with a note asking whether they would walk during the day over to my woodland pasture, where the soldiers had a barbecue before setting out for the Mexican war. The mother and Sylvia accepted. Our walk was a little overshadowed by their loss; and as I thoughtlessly described the gayety of that scene—the splendid young fellows dancing in their bright uniforms, and now and then pausing to wipe their foreheads, the speeches, the cheering, the dinner under the trees, and, a few days later, the tear-dimmed eyes, the hand-wringing and embracing, and at last the marching proudly away, each with a Bible in his pocket, and many never, never to return—I was sorry that I had not foreseen the sacred chord I was touching. But it made good friends of us more quickly, and they were well-bred, so that we returned to all appearance in gay spirits. The elder daughter came to meet us, and went at once silently to her mother's side, as though she had felt the separation. I wondered whether she had declined to go because of the memory of her father. As we passed my front gate, I asked them to look at my flowers. The mother praised also the cabbages, thus showing an admirably balanced mind; the little Sylvia fell in love with a vine-covered arbor; the elder daughter appeared to be secretly watching the many birds about the grounds, but when I pointed out several less-known species, she lost interest.

What surprises most is that they are so refined and intelligent. It is greatly to be feared that we Kentuckians in this part of the State are profoundly ignorant as to the people in other parts. I told Mrs. Walters this, and she, seeing that I am beginning to like them, is beginning to like them herself. Dear Mrs. Walters! Her few ideas are like three or four marbles on a level floor: they have no power to move themselves, but roll equally well in any direction you push them.

This afternoon I turned a lot of little town boys into my strawberry bed, and now it looks like a field that had been harrowed and rolled. I think they would gladly have pulled up some of the plants to see whether there might not be berries growing on the roots.

It is unwise to do everything that you can for people at once; for when you can do nothing more, they will say you are no longer like yourself, and turn against you. So I have meant to go slowly with the Cobbs in my wish to be neighborly, and do not think that they could reasonably be spoiled on one dish of strawberries in three weeks. But the other evening Mrs. Cobb sent over a plate of golden sally-lunn on a silver waiter, covered with a snow-white napkin; and acting on this provocation, I thought they could be trusted with a basket of cherries.

So next morning, in order to save the ripening fruit on a rather small tree of choice variety, I thought I should put up a scarecrow, and to this end rummaged a closet for some last winter's old clothes. These I crammed with straw, and I fastened the resulting figure in the crotch of the tree, tying the arms to the adjoining limbs, and giving it the dreadful appearance of shouting, "Keep out of here, you rascals, or you'll get hurt!" And, in truth, it did look so like me that I felt a little uncanny about it myself.

Returning home late, I went at once to the tree, where I found not a quart of cherries, and the servants told of an astonishing thing: that no sooner had the birds discovered who was standing in the tree, wearing the clothes in which he used to feed them during the winter, than the news spread like wildfire to the effect that he had climbed up there and was calling out: "Here is the best tree, fellows! Pitch in and help yourselves!" So that the like of the chattering and fetching away was never seen before. This was the story; but little negroes love cherries, and it is not incredible that the American birds were assisted in this instance by a large family of fat young African spoon-bills.

Anxious to save another tree, and afraid to use more of my own clothes, I went over to Mrs. Walters, and got from her an old bonnet and veil, a dress and cape, and a pair of her cast-off yellow gaiters. These garments I strung together and prepared to look life-like, as nearly as a stuffing of hay would meet the inner requirements of the case. I then seated the dread apparition in the fork of a limb, and awaited results. The first thief was an old jay, who flew towards the tree with his head turned to one side to see whether any one was overtaking him. But scarcely had he alighted when he uttered a scream of horror that was sickening to hear, and dropped on the grass beneath, after which he took himself off with a silence and speed that would have done credit to a passenger-pigeon. That tree was rather avoided for some days, or it may have been let alone merely because others were ripening; so that Mrs. Cobb got her cherries, and I sent Mrs. Walters some also for the excellent loan of her veil and gaiters.

As the days pass I fall in love with Sylvia, who has been persuaded to turn my arbor into a reading-room, and is often to be found there of mornings with one of Sir Walter's novels. Sometimes I leave her alone, sometimes lie on the bench facing her, while she reads aloud, or, tiring, prattles. Little half-fledged spirit, to whom the yard is the earth and June eternity, but who peeps over the edge of the nest at the chivalry of the ages, and fancies that she knows the world. The other day, as we were talking, she tapped the edge of her Ivanhoe with a slate-pencil— for she is also studying the Greatest Common Divisor—and said, warningly, "You must not make epigrams; for if you succeeded you would be brilliant, and everything brilliant is tiresome."

"Who is your authority for that epigram, Miss Sylvia?" I said, laughing.

"Don't you suppose that I have any ideas but what I get from books?"

"You may have all wisdom, but those sayings proceed only from experience."

"I have my intuitions; they are better than experience."

"If you keep on, you will be making epigrams presently, and then I shall find you tiresome, and go away."

"You couldn't. I am your guest. How unconventional: I am to come over and sit in your arbor! But it is Georgiana's fault."

"Did she tell you to come?"

"No; but she didn't keep me from coming. Whenever any one of us does anything improper we always say to each other, 'It's Georgiana's fault. She ought not to have taught us to be so simple and unconventional.'"

"And is she the family governess?"

"She governs the family. There doesn't seem to be any real government, but we all do as she says. You might think at first that Georgiana was the most light-headed member of the family, but she isn't. She's deep. I'm shallow in comparison with her. She calls me sophisticated, and introduces me as the elder Miss Cobb, and says that if I don't stop reading Scott's novels and learn more arithmetic she will put white caps on me, and make me walk to church in carpet slippers and with grandmother's stick."

"But you don't seem to have stopped, Miss Sylvia."

"No; but I'm stopping. Georgiana always gives us time, but we get right at last. It was two years before she could make my brother go to West Point. He was wild and rough, and wanted to raise tobacco, and float with it down to New Orleans, and have a good time. Then when she had gotten him to go she was afraid he'd come back, and so she persuaded my mother to live here, where there isn't any tobacco, and where I could be sent to school. That took her a year, and now she is breaking up my habit of reading nothing but novels. She gets us all down in the end. One day when she and Joe were little children they were out at the wood-pile, and Georgiana was sitting on a log eating a jam biscuit, with her feet on the log in front of her. Joe had a hand-axe, and was chopping at anything till he caught sight of her feet. Then he went to the end of the log, and whistled like a steamboat, and began to hack down in that direction, calling out to her: 'Take your toes out of the way, Georgiana. I am coming down the river. The current is up and I can't stop.' 'My toes were there first,' said Georgiana, and went on eating her biscuit. 'Take them out of the way, I tell you,' he shouted as he came nearer, 'or they'll get cut off.' 'They were there first,' repeated Georgiana, and took another delicious nibble. Joe cut straight along, and went whack right into her five toes. Georgiana screamed with all her might, but she held her foot on the log, till Joe dropped the hatchet with horror, and caught her in his arms. 'Georgiana, I told you to take your toes away,' he cried; 'you are such a little fool,' and ran with her to the house. But she always had control over him after that."

To-day I saw Sylvia enter the arbor, and shortly afterwards I followed with a book.

"When you stop reading novels and begin to read history, Miss Sylvia, here is the most remarkable history of Kentucky that was ever written or ever will be. It is by my father's old teacher of natural history in Transylvania University, Professor Rafinesque, who also had a wonderful botanical garden on this side of the town; perhaps the first ever seen in this country."

"I know all about it," replied Sylvia, resenting this slight upon her erudition. "Geor-giana has my father's copy, and his was presented to him by Mr. Audubon."

"Audubon?" I said, with a doubt.

"Never heard of Audubon?" cried Sylvia, delighted to show up my ignorance.

"Only of the great Audubon, Miss Sylvia; the great, the very great Audubon."

"Well, this was the great, the very great Audubon. He lived in Henderson, and kept a corn-mill. He and my father were friends, and he gave my father some of his early drawings of Kentucky birds. Georgiana has them now, and that is where she gets her love of birds—from my father, who got his from the great, the very great Audubon."

"Would Miss Cobb let me see these drawings?" I asked, eagerly.

"She might; but she prizes them as much as if they were stray leaves out of the only Bible in the world."

As Sylvia turned inside out this pocket of her mind, there had dropped out a key to her sister's conduct. Now I understood her slighting attitude towards my knowledge of birds. But I shall feel some interest in Miss Cobb from this time on. I never dreamed that she could bring me fresh news of that rare spirit whom I have so wished to see, and for one week in the woods with whom I would give any year of my life. Are they possibly the Henderson family to whom Audubon intrusted the box of his original drawings during his absence in Philadelphia, and who let a pair of Norway rats rear a family in it, and cut to pieces nearly a thousand inhabitants of the air?

There are two more days of June. Since the talk with Sylvia I have called twice more upon the elder Miss Cobb. Upon reflection, it is misleading to refer to this young lady in terms so dry, stiff, and denuded; and I shall drop into Sylvia's form, and call her simply Georgiana. That looks better—Georgiana! It sounds well, too—Georgiana!

Georgiana, then, is a rather elusive character. The more I see of her the less I understand her. If your nature draws near hers, it retreats. If you pursue, it flies—a little frightened perhaps. If then you keep still and look perfectly safe, she will return, but remain at a fixed distance, like a bird that will stay in your yard, but not enter your house. It is hardly shyness, for she is not shy, but more, like some strain of wild nature in her that refuses to be domesticated. One's faith is strained to accept Sylvia's estimate that Georgiana is deep—she is so light, so airy, so playful. Sylvia is a demure little dove that has pulled over itself an owl's skin, and is much prouder of its wicked old feathers than of its innocent heart; but Georgiana—what is she? Secretly an owl with the buoyancy of a humming-bird? However, it's nothing to me. She hovers around her mother and Sylvia with a fondness that is rather beautiful. I did not mention the subject of Audubon and her father, for it is never well to let an elder sister know that a younger one has been talking about her. I merely gave her several chances to speak of birds, but she ignored them. As for me and my love of birds, such trifles are beneath her notice. I don't like her, and it will not be worth while to call again soon, though it would be pleasant to see those drawings.

This morning as I was accidentally passing under her window I saw her at it and lifted my hat. She leaned over with her cheek in her palm, and said, smiling,

"You mustn't spoil Sylvia!"

"What is my definite offence in that regard?"

"Too much arbor, too many flowers, too much fine treatment."

"Does fine treatment ever harm anybody? Is it not bad treatment that spoils people?"

"Good treatment may never spoil people who are old enough to know its rarity and value. But you say you are a student of nature; have you not observed that nature never lets the sugar get to things until they are ripe? Children must be kept tart."

"The next time that Miss Sylvia comes over, then, I am to give her a tremendous scolding and a big basket of green apples."

"Or, what is worse, suppose you encourage her to study the Greatest Common Divisor? I am trying to get her ready for school in the fall."

"Is she being educated for a teacher?"

"You know that Southern ladies never teach."

"Then she will never need the Greatest Common Divisor. I have known many thousands of human beings, and none but teachers ever have the least use for the Greatest Common Divisor."

"But she needs to do things that she dislikes. We all do."

I smiled at the memory of a self-willed little bare foot on a log years ago.

"I shall see that my grape arbor does not further interfere with Miss Sylvia's progress towards perfection."

"Why didn't you wish us to be your neighbors?"

"I didn't know that you were the right sort of people."

"Are we the right sort?"

"The value of my land has almost been doubled."

"It is a pleasure to know that you approve of us on those grounds. Will the value of our land rise also, do you think? And why do you suppose we objected to you as a neighbor?"

"I cannot imagine."

"The imagination can be cultivated, you know. Then tell me this: why do Kentuck-ians in this part of Kentucky think so much of themselves compared with the rest of the world?"

"Perhaps it's because they are Virginians. There may be various reasons."

"Do the people ever tell what the reasons are?"

"I have never heard one."

"And if we stayed here long enough, and imitated them very closely, do you suppose we would get to feel the same way?"

"I am sure of it."

"It must be so pleasant to consider Kentucky the best part of the world, and your part of Kentucky the best of the State, and your family the best of all the best families in that best part, and yourself the best member of your family. Ought not that to make one perfectly happy?"

"I have often observed that it seems to do so."

"It is delightful to remember that you approve of us. And we should feel so glad to be able to return the compliment. Good-bye!"

Any one would have to admit, however, that there is no sharpness in Georgiana's pleasantry. The child-nature in her is so sunny, sportive, so bent on harmless mischief. She still plays with life as a kitten with a ball of yarn. Some day Kitty will fall asleep with the Ball poised in the cup of one foot. Then, waking, when her dream is over, she will find that her plaything has become a rocky, thorny, storm-swept, immeasurable world, and that she, a woman, stands holding out towards it her imploring arms, and asking only for some littlest part in its infinite destinies.

After the last talk with Georgiana I felt renewed desire to see those Audubon drawings. So yesterday morning I sent over to her some things written by a Northern man, whom I call the young Audubon of the Maine woods. His name is Henry D. Thoreau, and it is, I believe, known only to me down here. Everything that I can find of his is as pure and cold and lonely as a wild cedar of the mountain rocks, standing far above its smokeless valley and hushed white river. She returned them to-day with word that she would thank me in person, and to-night I went over in a state of rather senseless eagerness.

Her mother and sister had gone out, and she sat on the dark porch alone. The things of Thoreau's have interested her, and she asked me to tell her all I knew of him, which was little enough. Then of her own accord she began to speak of her father and Audubon—of the one with the worship of love, of the other with the worship of greatness. I felt as though I were in a moonlit cathedral; for her voice, the whole revelation of her nature, made the spot so impressive and so sacred. She scarcely addressed me; she was communing with them. Nothing that her father told her regarding Audubon appears to have been forgotten; and, brought nearer than ever before to that lofty, tireless spirit in its wanderings through the Kentucky forests, I almost forgot her to whom I was listening. But in the midst of it she stopped, and it was again kitten and yarn. I left quite as abruptly. Upon my soul, I believe that Georgiana doesn't think me worth talking to seriously.

VII

JULY has dragged like a log across a wet field.

There was the Fourth, which is always the grandest occasion of the year with us. Society has taken up Sylvia and rejected Georgiana; and so with its great gallantry, and to her boundless delight, Sylvia was invited to sit with a bevy of girls in a large furniture wagon covered with flags and bunting. The girls were to be dressed in white, carry flowers and flags, and sing "The Star-spangled Banner" in the procession, just before the fire-engine. I wrote a note to Georgiana, asking whether it would interfere with Sylvia's Greatest Common Divisor if I presented her with a profusion of elegant flowers on that occasion. Georgiana herself had equipped Sylvia with a truly exquisite silken flag on a silver staff; and as Sylvia both sang and waved with all her might, not only to keep up the Green River reputation in such matters, but with a mediaeval determination to attract a young man on the fire-engine behind, she quite eclipsed every other miss in the wagon, and was not even hoarse when persuaded at last to stop. So that several of the representatives of the other States voted afterwards in a special congress that she was loud, and in no way as nice as they had fancied, and that they ought never to recognize her again except in church and at funerals.

And then the month brought down from West Point the son of the family, who cut off—or cut at—Georgiana's toes, I remember. With him a sort of cousin, who lives in New York State; and after a few days of toploftical strutting around town, and a pusillanimous crack or two over the back-garden fence at my birds, they went away again, to the home of this New York cousin, carrying Georgiana with them to spend the summer.

Nothing has happened since. Only Sylvia and I have been making hay while the sun shines—or does not shine, if one chooses to regard Georgiana's absence in that cloudy fashion. Sylvia's ordinary armor consists of a slate-pencil for a spear, a slate for a shield, and a volume of Sir Walter for a battle-axe. Now and then I have found her sitting alone in the arbor with the drooping air of Lucy Ashton beside the fountain; and she would be better pleased if I met her clandestinely there in cloak and plume with the deadly complexion of Ravenswood.

The other day I caught her toiling at something, and she admitted being at work on a poem which would be about half as long as the "Lay of the Last Minstrel." She read me the opening lines, after that bland habit of young writers; and as nearly as I recollect, they began as follows:

"I love to have gardens, I love to have plants, I love to have air, and I love to have ants."

When not under the spell of mediaeval chivalry she prattles needlessly of Georgiana, early life, and their old home in Henderson. Although I have pointed out to her the gross impropriety of her conduct, she has persisted in reading me some of Georgiana's letters, written from the home of that New York cousin, whose mother they are now visiting. I didn't like him particularly. Sylvia relates that he was a favorite of her father's.

The dull month passes to-day. One thing I have secretly wished to learn: did her brother out Georgiana's toes entirely off?

IN August the pale and delicate poetry of the Kentucky land makes itself felt as silence and repose. Still skies, still woods, still sheets of forest water, still flocks and herds, long lanes winding without the sound of a traveller through fields of the universal brooding stillness. The sun no longer blazing, but muffled in a veil of palest blue. No more black clouds rumbling and rushing up from the horizon, but a single white one brushing slowly against the zenith like the lost wing of a swan. Far beneath it the silver-breasted hawk, using the cloud as his lordly parasol. The eagerness of spring gone, now all but incredible as having ever existed; the birds hushed and hiding ; the bee, so nimble once, fallen asleep over his own cider-press in the shadow of the golden apple. From the depths of the woods may come the notes of the cuckoo; but they strike the air more and more slowly, like the clack, clack, clack of a distant wheel that is being stopped at the close of harvest. The whirring wings of the locust let themselves go in one long wave of sound, passing into silence. All nature is a vast sacred goblet, filling drop by drop to the brim, and not to be shaken. But the stalks of the later flowers begin to be stuffed with hurrying bloom lest they be too late; and the nighthawk rapidly mounts his stairway of flight higher and higher, higher and higher, as though he would rise above the warm white sea of atmosphere and breathe in cold ether.

Always in August my nature will go its own way and seek its own peace. I roam solitary, but never alone, over this rich pastoral land, crossing farm after farm, and keeping as best I can out of sight of the laboring or loitering negroes. For the sight of them ruins every landscape, and I shall never feel myself free till they are gone. What if they sing? The more is the pity that any human being could be happy enough to sing so long as he was a slave in any thought or fibre of his nature.

Sometimes it is through the after-math of fat wheat-fields, where float like myriad little nets of silver gauze the webs of the crafty weavers, and where a whole world of winged small folk flit from tree-top to tree-top of the low weeds. They are all mine—these Kentucky wheat-fields. After the owner has taken from them his last sheaf I come in and gather my harvest also—one that he did not see, and doubtless would not begrudge me— the harvest of beauty. Or I walk beside tufted aromatic hemp-fields, as along the shores of softly foaming emerald seas; or past the rank and file of fields of Indian-corn, which stand like armies that had gotten ready to march, but been kept waiting for further orders, until at last the soldiers had gotten tired, as the gayest will, of their yellow plumes and green ribbons, and let their big hands fall heavily down at their sides. There the white and the purple morning-glories hang their long festoons and open to the soft midnight winds their elfin trumpets.

This year as never before I have felt the beauty of the world. And with the new brightness in which every common scene has been apparelled there has stirred within me a need of human companionship unknown in the past. It is as if Nature had spread out her last loveliness and said: "See! You have before you now all that you can ever get from me! It is not enough. Realize this in time. I am your Mother. Love me as a child. But remember! such love can be only a little part of your life."

Therefore I have spent the month restless, on the eve of change, drawn to Nature, driven from her. In September it will be different, for then there are more things to do on my small farm, and I see people on account of my grapes and pears. My malady this August has been an idle mind—so idle that a letter from Georgian a seems its main event. This was written from the old home of Audubon on the Hudson, whither they had gone sight-seeing. It must have been to her much like a pilgrimage to a shrine. She wrote informally, telling me about the place and enclosing a sprig of cedar from one of the trees in the yard. Her mind was evidently overflowing on the subject. It was rather pleasant to have the overflow turned my way. I shall plant the cedar where it will stay always green.

I saw Georgiana once more before her leaving. The sudden appearance of her brother and cousin, and the news that she would return with them for the summer, spurred me up to make another attempt at those Audubon drawings.

How easy it was to get them! It is what a man thinks a woman will be willing to do that she seldom does. But she made a confession. When she first found that I was a smallish student of birds, she feared I would not like Audubon, since men so often sneer at those who do in a grand way what they can do only in a poor one. I had another revelation of Georgiana's more serious nature, which is always aroused by the memory of her father. There is something beautiful and steadfast in this girl's soul. In our hemisphere vines climb round from left to right; if Georgiana loved you she would, if bidden, reverse every law of her nature for you as completely as a vine that you had caused to twine from right to left.

Sylvia enters school the 1st of September, and Georgiana is to be at home then to see to that. How surely she drives this family before her—and with as gentle a touch as that of a slow south wind upon the clouds.

Those poor first drawings of Audubon! He succeeded; we study his early failures. The world never studies the failures of those who do not succeed in the end.

The birds are moulting. If man could only moult also—his mind once a year its errors, his heart once a year its useless passions! How fine we should all look if every August the old plumage of our natures would drop out and be blown away, and fresh quills take the vacant places! But we have one set of feathers to last us through our threescore years and ten—one set of spotless feathers, which we are told to keep spotless through all our lives in a dirty world. If one gets broken, broken it stays; if one gets blackened, nothing will cleanse it. No doubt we shall all fly home at last, like a flock of pigeons that were once turned loose snow-white from the sky, and made to descend and fight one another and fight everything else for a poor living amid soot and mire. If then the hand of the unseen Fancier is stretched forth to draw us in, how can he possibly smite any one of us, or cast us away, because we came back to him black and blue with bruises and besmudged and bedraggled past all recognition?

IX

TO-DAY, the 7th of September, I made a discovery. The pair of red-birds that built in my cedar-trees last winter got duly away with the brood. Several times during summer rambles I cast my eye about, but they were not to be seen. Early this afternoon I struck out across the country towards a sinkhole in a field two miles away, some fifty yards in diameter, very deep, and enclosed by a fence. A series of these circular basins, at regular distances apart, runs across the country over there, suggesting the remains of ancient earth-works. The bottom had dropped out of this one, probably communicating with the many caves that are characteristic of this blue limestone.

Within the fence everything is an impenetrable thicket of weeds and vines—blackberry, thistle, ironweed, pokeweed,' elder, golden-rod. As I drew near, I saw two or three birds dive down, with the shy way they have at this season; and when I came to the edge, everything was quiet. But I threw a stone at a point where the tangle was deep, and there was a great flattering and scattering of the pretenders.

And then occurred more than I had looked for. The stone had hardly struck the brush when what looked like a tongue of vermilion flame leaped forth near by, and, darting across, stuck itself out of sight in the green vines on the opposite slope. A male and a female cardinal flew up also, balancing themselves on sprays of the blackberry, and uttering excitedly their quick call-notes. I whistled to the male as I had been used, and he recognized me by shooting up his crest and hopping to nearer twigs with louder inquiry. All at once, as if an idea had struck him, he sprang across to the spot where the first frightened male had disappeared. I could still hear him under the vines, and presently he reappeared and flew up into a locust-tree on the farther edge of the basin, followed by the other. What had taken place or took place then I do not know; but I wished he might be saying: "My son, that man over there is the one who was very-good to your mother and me last winter, and who owns the tree you were born in. I have warned you, of course, never to trust Man; but I would advise you, when you have found your sweetheart, to give him a trial, and take her to his cedar-trees."

If he said anything like this, it certainly had a terrible effect on the son; for, having mounted rapidly to the tree-top, he clove the blue with his scarlet wings as though he were flying from death. I lost sight of him over a corn-field.

One fact pleased me: the father returned to his partner under the briers, for he is not of the lower sort who forget the mother when the children are reared. They hold faithfully together during the ever more silent, ever more shadowy autumn days; his warming breast is close to hers through frozen winter nights; and if they both live to see another May she is still all the world to him, and woe to any brilliant vagabond who should warble a wanton love-song under her holy windows.

Georgiana returned the last of August. The next morning she was at her window, looking across into my yard. I was obliged to pass that way, and welcomed her gayly, expressing my thanks for the letter.

"I had to come back, you see," she said, with calm simplicity. I lingered awkwardly, stripping upward the stalks of some weeds.

"Very few Kentucky birds are migratory,"

I replied at length, with desperate brilliancy and an overwhelming grimace.

"I shall go back some time—to stay," she said, and turned away with a parting faintest smile.

Is that West Point brother giving trouble? If so, the sooner a war breaks out and he gets killed, the better. One thing is certain: if, for the next month, fruit and flowers will give Georgiana any pleasure, she shall have a good deal of pleasure. She is so changed! But why need I take on about it?

They have been cleaning out a drain under the streets along the Town Fork of Elkhorn, and several people are down with fever.

NEW-YEAR'S night again, and bitter cold.

When I forced myself away from my fire before dark, and ran down to the stable to see about feeding and bedding the horses and cows, every beast had its head drawn in towards its shoulders, and looked at me with the dismal air of saying, "Who is tempering the wind now?" The dogs in the kennel, with their noses between their hind-legs, were shivering under their blankets and straw like a nest of chilled young birds. The fowls on the roost were mere white and blue puffs of feathers. Nature alone has the making of her creatures; why doesn't she make them comfortable?

After supper old Jack and Dilsy came in, and standing against the wall with their arms folded, told me more of what happened after I got sick. That was about the middle of September, and it is only two weeks since I became well enough to go in and out through all sorts of weather.

It was the middle of September then, my servants said, and as within a week after taking the fever I was very ill, a great many people came out to inquire for me. Some of these, walking around the garden, declared it was a pity for such fruit and flowers to be wasted, and so helped themselves freely every time. The old doctor, who always fears for my health at this season, stopped by nearly every day to repeat how he had warned me, and always walked back to his gig in a roundabout way, which required him to pass a favorite tree; and once he was so indignant to find several other persons gathered there, and mournfully enjoying the last of the fruit as they predicted I would never get well, that he came back to the house—with two pears in each duster pocket and one in his mouth—and told Jack it was an outrage. The preacher, likewise, who appears in the spring-time, one afternoon knocked reproachfully at the front door and inquired whether I was in a condition to be reasoned with. In his hand he carried a nice little work-basket, which may have been brought along to catch his prayers; but he took it home piled with grapes.

And then they told me, also, how many a good and kind soul came with hushed footsteps and low inquiries, turning away sometimes with brightened faces, sometimes with rising tears—often people to whom I had done no kindness or did not even know; how others, whom I had quarrelled with or did not like, forgot the poor puny quarrels and the dislike, and begged to do for me whatever they could; how friends went softly around the garden, caring for a flower, putting a prop under a too heavily-laden limb, or climbing on step-ladders to tie sacks around the finest bunches of grapes, with the hope that I might be well in time to eat them—touching nothing themselves, having no heart to eat; how dear, dear ones would never leave me day or night; how a good doctor wore himself out with watching, and a good pastor sent up for me his spotless prayers; and at last, when I began to mend, how from far and near there poured in flowers and jellies and wines, until, had I been the multitude by the Sea of Galilee, there must have been baskets to spare. God bless them! God bless them all! And God forgive us all the blindness, the weakness, and the cruelty with which we judge each other when we are in health.

This and more my beloved old negroes told me a few hours ago, as I sat in deep comfort and bright health again before my blazing hickories; and one moment we were in laughter and the next in tears—as is the strange life we live. This is a gay household now, and Dilsy cannot face me without a fleshly earthquake of laughter that I have become such a high-tempered tiger about punctual meals.

In particular, my two nearest neighbors were much at odds as to which had better claim to nurse me; so that one day Mrs. Walters, able to endure it no longer, thrust Mrs. Cobb out of the house by the shoulder-blades, locked the door on her, and then opened the shutters and scolded her out of the window.

One thing I miss. My servants have never called the name of Georgiana. The omission is unnatural, and must be intentional. Of course I have not asked whether she showed any care; but that little spot of silence affects me as the sight of a tree remaining leafless in the woods where everything else is turning green.

XI

TO-DAY I was standing at a window, looking out at the aged row of cedars, now laden with snow, and thinking of Horace and Soracte. Suddenly, beneath a jutting pinnacle of white boughs which left under themselves one little spot of green, I saw a cardinal hop out and sit full-breasted towards me. The idea flashed through my mind that this might be that shyest, most beautiful fellow whom I had found in September, and whom I tried to make out as the son of my last winter's pensioner. At least he has never lived in my yard before; for when, to test his shyness, I started to raise the window-sash, at the first noise of it he was gone. My birds are not so afraid of me.

I must get on better terms with this stranger.

Mrs. Walters over for a while afterwards. I told her of my fancy that this bird was one of last summer's brood, and that he appeared a trifle larger than any male I had ever seen. She said of course. Had I not fed the parents all last winter? When she fed her hens, did they not lay bigger eggs? Did not bigger eggs contain bigger chicks? Did not bigger chicks become bigger hens, again? According to Mrs. Walters, a single winter's feeding of hot corn-meal, scraps of bacon, and pods of red pepper will all but bring about a variation of species; and so if the assumed rate at which I am now going were kept up a hundred years, my cedar-trees might be full of a race of red-birds as large and as fat as geese.

Standing towards sundown at another window, I saw Georgiana sewing at hers, as I have seen her every day since I got out of bed. Why should she sew so much? There is a servant also; and they sew, sew, sew, as if eternal sewing were eternal happiness, eternal salvation. The first day she sprang up, letting her work roll off her lap, and waved her handkerchief inside the panes, and smiled with what looked to me like radiant pleasure that I was well again. I was weak and began to tremble, and, going back to the fireside, lay back in my chair with a beating of the heart that was a warning. Since then she has recognized me by only a quiet kindly smile. Why has no one ever called her name? I believe Mrs. Walters knows. She comes nowadays as if to tell something, and goes away with a struggle that she has not told it. But a secret can no more stay in the depths of Mrs. Walters's mind than cork at the bottom of water; some day I shall see this mystery riding on the surface.

XII

YES, she knew; while unconscious I talked of Georgiana, of being in love with her. Mrs. Walters added, sadly, that Georgiana came home in the fall engaged to that New York cousin. Hence the sewing—he is to marry her in June.

I am not in love with her. It is now four weeks since hearing this conventional fiction, and every day I have been perfectly able to repeat: "I am not in love with Georgiana!" There was one question which I put severely to Mrs. Walters: Had she told Georgiana of my foolish talk? She shook her head violently, and pressed her lips closely together, suggesting how impossible it would be for the smallest monosyllable in the language to escape by that channel; but she kept her eyes wide open, and the truth issued from them, as smoke in a hollow tree, if stopped in at a lower hole, simply rises and comes out at a higher one. "You should have shut your eyes also," I said. "You have told her every word of it, and the Lord only knows how much more."

This February has let loose its whole pack of grizzly sky-hounds. Unbroken severe weather. Health has not returned as rapidly as was promised, and I have not ventured outside the yard. But it is a pleasure to chronicle the beginning of an acquaintanceship between his proud eminence the young cardinal and myself. For a long time he would have naught to do with me, fled as I approached, abandoned the evergreens altogether and sat on the naked tree-tops, as much as threatening to quit the place altogether if I did not leave him in peace.

Surely he is the shyest of his kind, and, to my fancy, the most beautiful; and therefore Nature seems to have stored him with extra caution towards his archenemy.

But in the old human way I have taken advantage of his necessities. The north wind has been my friend against him. I have called in the aid of sleets and snows, have besieged him in his white castle behind the glittering array of his icicles with threats of starvation. So one day, dropping like a glowing coal down among the other birds, he snatched a desperate hasty meal from the public poor-house table that I had spread under the trees.

It is the first surrender that decides. Since then some progress has been made in winning his confidence, but the struggle going on in his nature is plain enough still. At times he will rush away from me in utter terror; at others he lets me draw a little nearer, a little nearer, without moving from a limb; and now, after a month of persuasion, he begins to discredit the experience which he has inherited from centuries upon centuries of ancestors. In all that I have done I have tried to say to him: "Don't judge me by mankind in general. With me you are safe. I pledge myself to defend you from enemies, high and low."

This had not escaped the notice of Georgiana at the window, and more than once she had let her work drop to watch my patient progress and to bestow upon me a rewarding smile. Is there nearly always sadness in it, or is the sadness in my eyes? If Georgiana's brother is giving her trouble, I'd like to take a hand-axe to his feet. I suppose I shall never know whether he cut her foot in two. She carries the left one a little peculiarly ; but so many women do that.

Sometimes, when the day's work is over and the servant is gone, Georgiana comes to the window and looks away towards the sunsets of winter, her hands clasped behind her back, her motionless figure in relief against the darkness within, her face white and still. Being in the shadow of my own room, so that she could not see me, and knowing that I ought not to do it, but unable to resist, I have softly taken up the spy-glass which I use in the study of birds, and have drawn Georgiana's face nearer to me, holding it there till she turns away. I have noted the traces of pain, and once the tears which she could not keep back and was too proud to heed. Then I have sat before my flickering embers, with I know not what all but ungovernable yearning to be over there in the shadowy room with her, and, whether she would or not, to fold my arms around her, and, drawing her face against mine, whisper: "What is it, Georgiana? And why must it be?"

XIII

THE fountains of the great deep opened. A new heaven, a new earth. Georgiana has broken her engagement with her cousin. Mrs. Cobb let it out in the strictest confidence to Mrs. Walters. Mrs. Walters, with stricter confidence still, has told me only.

The West-Pointer had been writing for some months in regard to the wild behavior of his cousin. This grew worse, and the crisis came. Georgiana snapped her thread and put up her needle. He travelled all the way down here to implore. I met him at the gate as he left the house—a fine, straight, manly, handsome young fellow, with his face pale with pain, and his eyes flashing with anger—and bade him a long, affectionate, inward God-speed as he hurried away. It was her father's influence. He had always wished for this union. Ah, the evils that come to the living from the wrongful wishes of the dead! Georgiana is so happy now, since she has been forced to free herself, that spring in this part of the United States seems to have advanced about half a month.

"What on earth will she do with all those clothes?" inquired Mrs. Walters the other night, eying me with curious impressiveness.

"They ought to be hanged," I said, promptly.

There is a young scapegrace who passes my house morning and evening with his cows. He has the predatory instincts of that being who loves to call himself the image of his Maker, and more than once has given annoyance, especially last year, when he robbed a damson-tree of a brood of Baltimore orioles.

This winter and spring his friendly interest in my birds has increased, and several times I have caught him skulking among the pines. Last night what should I stumble on but a trap, baited and sprung, under the cedar-tree in which the cardinal roosts. I was up before daybreak this morning. A while after the waking of the birds here comes my young bird-thief, creeping rapidly to his trap. As he stooped I had him by the collar, and within the next five minutes I must have set up in his nervous system a negative disposition to the caging of red-birds that will descend as a positive tendency to all the generations of his offspring.

All day this meditated outrage has kept my blood up. Think of this beautiful cardinal beating his heart out against maddening bars, or caged for life in some dark city street, lonely, sick, and silent, bidden to sing joyously of that high world of light and liberty where once he sported! Think of the exquisite refinement of cruelty in wishing to take him on the eve of May!

It is hardly a fancy that something as loyal as friendship has sprung up between this bird and me. I accept his original shyness as a mark of his finer instincts; but, like the nobler natures, when once he found it possible to give his confidence, how frankly and fearlessly has it been given. The other day, brilliant, warm, windless, I was tramping across the fields a mile from home, when I heard him on the summit of a dead sycamore, cleaving the air with stroke after stroke of his long melodious whistle, as with the swing of a silken lash. When I drew near he dropped down from bough to bough till he reached the lowest, a few feet from where I stood, and showed by every movement how glad he was to see me. We really have reached the understanding that the immemorial persecution of his race by mine is ended ; and now more than ever my fondness settles about him, since I have found his happiness plotted against, and have perhaps saved his very life. It would be easy to trap him. His eye should be made to distrust every well-arranged pile of sticks under which lurks a morsel.

To-night I called upon Georgiana and sketched the arrested tragedy of the morning. She watched me curiously, and then dashed into a little treatise on the celebrated friendships of man for the lower creatures, in fact and fiction, from camels down to white mice. Her father must have been a remarkably learned man. I didn't like this. It made me somehow feel as though I were one of Aesop's Fables, or were being translated into English as that old school-room horror of Androclus and the Lion. In the bottom of my soul I don't believe that Georgiana cares for birds, or knows the difference between a blackbird and a crow. I am going to send her a little story, "The Passion of the Desert." Mrs. Walters is now confident that Georgiana regrets having broken off her engagement. But then Mrs. Walters can be a great fool when she pats her whole mind to it.

XIV

IN April I commence to scratch and dig in my garden.

To-day, as I was raking off my strawberry bed, Georgiana, whom I have not seen since the night when she satirized me, called from the window:

"What are you going to plant this year?"

"Oh, a little of everything," I answered, under my hat. "What are you going to plant this year?"

"Are you going to have many strawberries?"

"It's too soon to tell: they haven't bloomed yet. It's too soon to tell when they do bloom. Sometimes strawberries are like women: Whole beds full of showy blossoms; but when the time comes to be ripe and luscious, you can't find them."

"Indeed."

"'Tis true, 'tis pity."

"I had always supposed that to a Southern gentleman woman was not a berry but a rose. What does he hunt for in woman as much as bloom and fragrance? But I don't belong to the rose-order of Southern women myself. Sylvia does. Why did you send me that story?"

"Didn't you like it?"

"No. A woman couldn't care for a story about a man and a tigress. Either she would feel that she was too much left out, or suspect that she was too much put in. The same sort of story about a lion and a woman— that would be better."

I raked in silence for a minute, and when I looked up Georgiana was gone. I remember her saying once that children should be kept tart; but now and then I fancy that she would like to keep even a middle-aged man in brine. Who knows but that in the end I shall sell my place to the Cobbs and move away?

Five more days of April, and then May! For the last half of this light-and-shadow month, when the clouds, like schools of changeable lovely creatures, seem to be playing and rushing away through the waters of the sun, life to me has narrowed more and more to the red-bird, who gets tamer and tamer with habit, and to Georgiana, who gets wilder and wilder with happiness. The bird fills the yard with brilliant singing; she fills her room with her low, clear songs, hidden behind the window-curtains, which are now so much oftener and so needlessly closed. I work myself nearly to death in my garden, but she does not open them. The other day the red-bird sat in a tree near by, and his notes floated out on the air like scarlet streamers. Georgian a was singing, so low that I was making no noise with my rake in order to hear ; and when he began, before I realized what I was doing, I had seized a brickbat and hurled it, barely missing him, and driving him away. He did not know what to make of it; neither did I; but as I raised my eyes I saw that Georgiana had opened the curtains to listen to him, and was closing them with her eyes on my face, and a look on hers that has haunted me ever since.

April the 26th. It's of no use. To-morrow night I will go to see Georgians, and ask her to marry me.

April 28th. Man that is born of woman is of few days and full of trouble. I am not the least sick, but I am not feeling at all well. So have made a will, and left everything to Mrs. Walters. She has been over five times to-day, and this evening sat by me a long time, holding my hand and smoothing my forehead, and urging me to try a cream poultice—a mustard-plaster—a bowl of gruel—a broiled chicken.

I believe Georgiana thinks I'll ask her again. Not if I lived by her through eternity I Thy rod and Thy staff—they comfort me.

XV

A POOR devil will ask a woman to marry him. She will refuse him. The day after she will meet him as serenely as if he had asked her for a pin.

It is now May 15th, and I have not spoken to Georgiana when I've had a chance. She has been entirely too happy, to judge from her singing, for me to get along with under the circumstances. But this morning, as I was planting a hedge inside my fence under her window, she leaned over and said, as though nothing were wrong between us, "What are you planting?"

I have sometimes thought that Georgiana can ask more questions than Socrates.

"A hedge"

"What for?"

"To grow."

"What do you want it to grow for?"

"My garden is too public. I wish to be protected from outsiders."

"Would it be the same thing if I were to nail up this window? That would be so much quicker. It will be ten years before your hedge is high enough to keep me from seeing you. And even then, you know, I could move up-stairs. But I am so sorry to be an outsider."

"I merely remarked that I was planting a hedge."

When Georgiana spoke again her voice was lowered: "Would you open a gateway for me into your garden, to be always mine, so that I might go out and come in, and never another human soul enter it?"

Now Jacob had often begged me to cut him a private gateway on that side of the garden, so that only he might come in and go out; and I had refused, since I did not wish him to get to me so easily with his complaints. Besides, a gate once opened, who may not use it? and I was indignant that Georgiana should lightly ask anything at my hands; therefore I looked quickly and sternly up at her and said, "I will not."

Afterwards the thought rushed over me that she had not spoken of any gateway through my garden fence, but of another one, mystical, hidden, infinitely more sacred. For her voice descended almost in a whisper, and her face, as she bent down towards me, had on it I know not what angelic expression. She seemed floating to me from heaven.

May 17th. To-day I put a little private gate through my fence under Georgiana's window, as a sign to her. Balaam's beast that I am! Yes, seven times more than the inspired ass.

As I passed to-day, I noticed Georgiana looking down at the gate that I made yesterday. She held a flower to her nose and eyes, but behind the leaves I detected that she was laughing.

"Good-morning!" she called to me. "What did you cut that ugly hole in your fence for?"

"That's not an ugly hole. That's a little private gateway."

"But what's the little private gateway for?"

"Oh, well! You don't understand these matters. I'll tell your mother."

"My mother is too old. She no longer stoops to such things. Tell me!"

"Impossible!"

"I'm dying to know!"

"What will you give me?"

"Anything—this flower!"

"But what would the flower stand for in that case? A little pri—"

"Nothing. Take it!" and she dropped it lightly on my face and disappeared. As I stood twirling it ecstatically under my nose, and wondering how I could get her to come back to the window, the edge of a curtain was lifted, and a white hand stole out and softly closed the shutters.

In the evening Sylvia went in to a concert of the school, which was to be held at the Court-house, a chorus of girls being impanelled in the jury-box, and the principal, who wears a little wig, taking her seat on the woolsack. I promised to have the very pick of the garden ready, and told Sylvia to come to the arbor the last thing before starting. She wore big blue rosettes in her hair, and at that twilight hour looked as lovely, soft, and pure as moonshine; so that I lost control of myself and kissed her twice—once for Georgiana and once for myself. Surely it must have been Sylvia's first experience. I hope so. Yet she passed through it with the composure of a graduate of several years' standing. But, then, women inherit a great stock of fortitude from their mothers in this regard, and perpetually add to it by their own dispositions. Ought I to warn Georgiana—good heavens! in a general way, of course—that Sylvia should be kept away from sugar, and well under the influence of vulgar fractions?

It made me feel uncomfortable to see her go tripping out of her front gate on the arm of a youth. Can it be possible that he would try to do what I did? Men differ so in their virtues, and are so alike in their transgressions. This forward gosling displayed white duck pantaloons, brandished pumps on his feet, which looked flat enough to have been webbed, and was scented as to his marital locks with a far-reaching pestilence of bergamot and cinnamon.

After they were gone I strolled back to my arbor and sat down amid the ruins of Sylvia's flowers. The night was mystically beautiful. The moon seemed to me to be softly stealing down the sky to kiss Endymion. I looked across towards Georgiana's window. She was there, and I slipped over and stood under it.

"Georgiana," I whispered, "were you, too, looking at the moon?"

"Part of the time," she said, sourly. "Isn't it permitted?"

"Sylvia left her scissors in the arbor, and I can't find them."

"She'll find them to-morrow."

"If they get wet, you know, they'll rust."

"I keep something to take rust off."

"Georgiana, I've got something to tell you about Sylvia."

"What? That you kissed her?"

"N—o! Not that, exactly!"

"Good-night!"

May 21st. Again I asked Georgiana to be mine. I am a perfect fool about her. But she's coming my way at last—God bless her!

May 24th. I renewed my suit to Georgiana.

May 27th. I besought Georgiana to hear me.

May 28th. For the last time I offered my hand in marriage to the elder Miss Cobb. Now I am done with her forever. I am no fool.

May 29th. Oh, damn Mrs. Walters!

XVI

THIS morning, the 3d of June, I went out to pick the first dish of strawberries for my breakfast. As I was stooping down I heard a timid, playful voice at the window like the echo of a year ago: "Are you the gardener?"

Since Georgiana will not marry me, if she would only let me alone!

"Old man, are you the gardener?"

"Yes, I'm the gardener. I know what you are."

"How much do you ask for your strawberries?"

"They come high. Nothing of mine is to be as cheap hereafter as it has been."

"I am so glad—for your sake. I should like to possess something of yours, but I suppose everything is too high now."

"Entirely too high!"

"If I only could have foreseen that there would be an increase of value! As for me, I have felt that I am getting cheaper lately. I may have to give myself away soon. If I only knew of some one who loved the lower animals."

"The fox, for instance?"

"Yes; do you know of any one who would accept the present of a fox?"

"Ahem! I wouldn't mind having a tame fox. I don't care much for wild foxes."

"Oh, this one would get tame—in time."

"I don't believe I know of any one just at present."

"Very well. Sylvia will get the highest mark in arithmetic. And Joe is distinguishing himself at West Point. That's what I wanted to tell you. I'll send you over the cream and sugar, and hope you will enjoy all your berries. We shall buy some in the market-house next week."

Later in the forenoon I sent the strawberries over to Georgiana. I have a variety that is the shape of the human heart, and when ripe it matches in color that brighter current of the heart through which runs the hidden history of our passions. All over the top of the dish I carefully laid these heart-shaped berries, and under the biggest one, at the very top, I slipped this little note: "Look at the shape of them, Georgiana! I send them all to you. They are perishable."

This afternoon Georgiana sent back the empty dish, and inside the napkin was this note: "They are exactly the shape and color of my emery needle-bag. I have been polishing my needles in it for many years."

Later, as I was walking to town, I met Georgiana and her mother coming out. No explanation had ever been made to the mother of that goose of a gate in our division fence; and as Georgiana had declined to accept the sign, I determined to show her that the gate could now stand for something else. So I said: "Mrs. Cobb, when you send your servants over for green corn, you can let them come through that little gate. It will be more convenient."

Only, I was so angry and confused that I called her Mrs. Corn, and said that when she sent her little Cobbs over . . . my green servants, etc.

After Georgiana's last treatment of me I resolved not to let her talk to me out of her window. So about nine o'clock this morning I took a negro boy and set him to picking the berries, while I stood by, directing him in a deep, manly voice as to the best way of managing that intricate business. Presently I heard Georgiana begin to sing to herself behind the curtains.

"Hurry up and fill that cup," I said to him, savagely. "And that will do this morning. You can go to the mill. The meal's nearly out."

When he was gone I called, in an undertone: "Georgiana! Come to the window! Please! Oh, Georgiana!"

But the song went on. What was the matter? I could not endure it. There was one way by which perhaps she could be brought. I whistled long and loud again and again. The curtains parted a little space.

"I was merely whistling to the bird? I said.

"I knew it," she answered, looking as I had never seen her. "Whenever you speak to him your voice is full of confidence and of love. I believe in it and like to hear it."

"What do you mean, Georgiana?" I cried, imploringly.

"Ah, Adam!" she said, with a rush of feeling. It was the first time she had ever called me by name. She bent her face down. Over it there passed a look of sweetness and sadness indescribably blended. "Ah, Adam! you have asked me many times to marry you! Make me believe once that you love me! Make me feel that I could trust myself to you for life!"

"What else can I do?" I answered, stirred to the deepest that was in me, throwing my arms backward, and standing with an open breast into which she might gaze.

And she did search my eyes and face in silence.

"What more," I cried again, "in God's name?"

She rested her face on her palm, looking thoughtfully across the yard. Over there the red-bird was singing. Suddenly she leaned down towards me. Love was on her face now. But her eyes held mine with the determination to wrest from them the last truth they might contain, and her voice trembled with doubt:

"Would you put the red-bird in a cage for me? Would you be willing to do that for me, Adam?".

At those whimsical, cruel words I shall never be able to reveal all that I felt—the surprise, the sorrow, the pain. Scenes of boyhood flashed through my memory. A conscience built up through years of experience stood close by me with admonition. I saw the love on her face, the hope with which she hung upon my reply, as though it would decide everything between us. I did not hesitate; my hands dropped to my side, the warmth died out of my heart as out of spent ashes, and I answered her, with cold reproach,

"I—will—not!"

The color died out of her face also. Her eyes still rested on mine, but now with pitying sadness.

"I feared it," she murmured, audibly, but to herself, and the curtains fell together.

Four days have passed. Georgiana has cast me off. Her curtains are closed except when she is not there. I have tried to see her; she excuses herself. I have written; my letters come back unread. I have lain in wait for her on the streets; she will not talk with me. The tie between us has been severed. With her it could never have been affection.

And for what? I ask myself over and over and over—for what? Was she jealous of the bird, and did she require that I should put it out of the way? Sometimes women do that. Did she take that means of forcing me to a test? Women do that. Did she wish to show her power over me, demanding the one thing she knew would be the hardest for me to grant? Women do that. Did she crave the pleasure of seeing me do wrong to humor her caprice? Women do that. But not one of these things can I even associate with the thought of Georgiana. I have sought in every way to have her explain, to explain myself. She will neither give nor receive an explanation.

I had supposed that her unnatural request would have been the end of my love, but it has not; that her treatment since would have fatally stung my pride, but it has not. I understand neither; forgive both; love her now with that added pain which comes from a man's discovering that the woman dearest to him must be pardoned—pardoned as long as he shall live.

Never since have I been able to look at the red-bird with the old gladness. He is the reminder of my loss. Reminder? Do I ever forget? Am I not thinking of that before his notes lash my memory at dawn? All day can they do more than furrow deeper the channel of unforgetfulness? Little does he dream what my friendship for him has cost me. But this solace I have at heart—that I was not even tempted to betray him.

Three days more have passed. No sign yet that Georgiana will relent soon or ever. Each day the strain becomes harder to bear. My mind has dwelt upon my last meeting with her, until the truth about it wavers upon my memory like vague, uncertain shadows. She doubted my love for her. What proof was it she demanded? I must stop looking at the red-bird, lying here and there under the trees, and listening to him as he sings above me. My eyes devour him whenever he crosses my path with an uncomprehended fascination that is pain. How gentle he has become, and how, without intending it, I have deepened the perils of his life by the very gentleness that I have brought upon him. Twice already the fate of his species has struck at him, but I have pledged myself to be his friend. This is his happiest season; a few days now, and he will hear the call of his young in the nest.

I shut myself in my workshop in the yard this morning. I did not wish my servants to know. In there I made a bird-trap such as I had often used when a boy. And late this afternoon I went to town and bought a bird-cage. I was afraid the merchant would misjudge me, and explained. He scanned my face silently. To-morrow I will snare the red-bird down behind the pines long enough to impress on his memory a lifelong suspicion of every such artifice, and then I will set him free again in his wide world of light. Above all things, I must see to it that he does not wound himself or have the least feather broken.

It is far past midnight now, and I have not slept or wished for slumber.

Constantly since darkness came on I have been watching Georgiana's window for the light of her candle, but there has been no kindly glimmer yet. The only radiance shed upon the gloom outside comes from the heavens. Great cage-shaped white clouds are swung up to the firmament, and within these pale, gentle, imprisoned lightnings flutter feebly to escape, fall back, rise, and try again and again, and fail.

. . . A little after dark this evening I carried the red-bird over to Georgiana. . .
.

I have seen her so little of late that I did not know she had been away from home for days. But she was expected to-night, or, at furthest, to-morrow morning. I left the bird with the servant at the door, who could hardly believe what he saw. As I passed out of my front gate on my way there, the boy who returns about that time from the pasture for his cows joined me as I hurried along, attracted by the fluttering of the bird in the cage.

"Is it the red-bird? I tried to ketch him once," he said, with entire forgiveness of me, as having served him right, "but I caught something else. I'll never forget that whipping. Oh, but wouldn't I like to have him! Mr. Moss, you wouldn't mind my trying to ketch one of them little bits o'brown fellows, would you, that hops around under them pine-trees? They ain't no account to nobody. Oh my! but wouldn't I like to have him! May I bring my trap some time, and will you help me to ketch one o'them little bits o'brown ones? You can beat me ketchin' 'em!"

Several times to-night I have gone across and listened under Georgiana's window. The servant must have set the cage in her room, for, as I listened, I am sure I heard the red-bird beating his head and breast against the wires. Awhile ago I went again, and did not hear him. I waited a long time. . . . He may be quieted. . . .

Ah, if any one had said to me that I would ever do what I have done, with what full, deep joy could I have throttled the lie in his throat! I put the trap under one of the trees where I have been used to feed him. When it fell he was not greatly frightened. He clutched the side of it, and looked out at me. My own mind supplied his words: "Help! I'm caught! Take me out! You promised!" When I transferred him to the cage, for a moment his confidence lasted still. He mounted the perch, shook his plumage, and spoke out bravely and cheerily. Then all at once came on the terror.

The dawn came on this morning with its old splendor. The birds in my yard, as of old, poured forth their songs. But those loud, long, clear, melodious, deep-hearted, passionate, best-loved notes! As the chorus swelled from shadowy shrubs and vines to the sparkling tree-tops I listened for some sound from Georgiana's room, but over there I saw only the soft, slow flapping of the white curtains like signals of distress.

Towards ten o'clock, wandering restless, I snatched up a book, which I had no wish to read, and went to the arbor where I had so often discoursed to Sylvia about children's cruelty to birds. Through the fluttering leaves the sunlight dripped as a weightless shower of gold, and the long pendants of young fruit swayed gently in their cool waxen greenness. Where some rotting planks crossed the top of the arbor a blue-jay sat on her coarse nest; and presently the mate flew to her with a worm, and then talked to her in a low voice, as much as saying that they mast now leave the place forever. I was thinking how love softens even the voice of this file-throated screamer, when along the garden walk came the rustle of a woman's clothes, and, springing up, I stood face to face with Georgiana.

"What have you done?" she implored.

"What have you done?" I answered as quickly.

"Oh, Adam, Adam! You have killed it! How could you? How could you?"

"... Is he dead, Georgiana? Is he dead?..."

I forgot everything else, and pulling my hat down over my eyes, turned from her in the helpless shock of silence that came with those irreparable words.

Then, in ungovernable anger, suffering, remorse, I turned upon her where she sat: "It is you who killed him! Why do you come here to blame me? And now you pretend to be sorry. You felt no pity when pity would have done some good. Trifler! Hypocrite!"

"It is false!" she cried, her words flashing from her whole countenance, her form drawn up to repel the shock of the blow.

"Did you not ask me for him?"

"No!"

"Oh, deny it all! It is a falsehood—invented by me on the spot. You know nothing of it! You did not ask me to do this! And when I have yielded, you have not run to reproach me here and to cry, 'How could you? How could you?' "

"No! No! Every word of it—"

"Untruth added to it all! Oh, that I should have been so deceived, blinded, taken in!"

"Adam!"

"Lovely innocence! It is too much! Go away!"

"I will not stand this any longer!" she cried. "I will go away; but not till I have told you why I have acted as I have."

"It is too late for that! I do not care to hear!"

"Then you shall hear!" she replied. "You shall know that it is because I have believed you capable of speaking to me as you have just spoken; believed you at heart unsparing and unjust. You think I asked you to do what you have done? No! I asked you whether you would be willing to do it; and when you said you would not, I saw then—by your voice, your eyes, your whole face and manner—that you would. Saw it as plainly at that moment, in spite of your denial, as I see it now—the cruelty in you, the unfaithfulness, the willingness to betray. It was for this reason—not because I heard you refuse, but because I saw you consent—that I could not forgive you."

She paused abruptly and looked across into my face. What she may now have read in it I do not know. Then anger swept her on:

"How often had I not heard you bitter and contemptuous towards people because they are treacherous, cruel! How often have you talked of your love of nature, of our inhumanity towards lower creatures! But what have you done?

"You set your fancy upon one of these creatures, lie in wait for it, beset it with kindness, persevere in overcoming its wildness. You are amused, delighted, proud of your success. One day—you remember?—it sang as you had always wished to hear it. It annoyed you, and you threw a stone at it. With a little less angry aim you would have killed it. I have never seen anything more inhuman. How do I know that some day you would not be tired of me, and throw a stone at me? When a woman submits to this once, she will have them thrown at her whenever she sings at the wrong time, and she will never know when the right time is.

"Then you thought you were asked to sacrifice it, and now you have done that. How do I know that some day you might not be tempted to sacrifice me?" She paused, her voice breaking, and remained silent, as if unable to get beyond that thought.

"If you have finished," I said, very quietly, "I have something to say to you, and we need not meet after this.

"I trapped the bird; you trapped me. I understood you to ask something of me, to cast me off when I refused it. Such was my faith in you that beneath your words I did not look for a snare. How hard it was for me to forgive you what you asked is my own affair now; but forgive you I did. How hard it was to grant it, that also is now, and will always be, my own secret. I beg you merely to believe this: knowing it to be all that you have described—and far more than you can ever understand— still, I did it. Had you demanded of me something worse, I should have granted that. If you think a man will not do wrong for a woman, you are mistaken. If you think men always love the wrong that they do for the women whom they love, you are mistaken again.

"You have held up my faults to me. I knew them before. I have not loved them. Do not think that I am trying to make a virtue out of anything I say; but in all my thoughts of you there has been no fault of yours that I have not hidden from my sight, and have not resolved as best I could never to see. Yet do not dream that I have found you faultless.

"You fear I might sacrifice you to something else. It is possible. Every man resists temptation only to a certain point; every man has his price. It is a risk you will run with any.

"If you doubt that a man is capable of sacrificing one thing that he loves to another that he loves more, tempt him, lie in wait for his weakness, ensnare him in the toils of his greater passion, and learn the truth.

"I make no defence—believe all that you say. But had you loved me, I might have been all this, and it would have been nothing."

With this I walked slowly out of the arbor, but Georgiana stood beside me. Her light touch was on my arm.

"Let me see things clearly!"

"You have a lifetime in which to see things clearly," I answered. "How can that concern me now?" And I passed on into the house.

During the morning I wandered restless. For a while I lay on the grass down behind the pines. How deep and clear are the covered springs of memory! All at once it was a morning in my boyhood on my father's farm. I, a little Saul of Tarsus among the birds, was on my way to the hedge-rows and woods, as to Damascus, breathing out threatenings and slaughter. Then suddenly the childish miracle, which no doubt had been preparing silently within my nature, wrought itself out; for from the distant forest trees, from the old orchard, from thicket and fence, from the wide green meadows, and down out of the depths of the blue sky itself, a vast chorus of innocent creatures sang to my newly opened ears the same words: "Why persecutest thou me?" One sang it with indignation; another with remonstrance; still another with resignation; others yet with ethereal sadness or wild elusive pain. Once more the house-wren met me at the rotting gate-post, and cried aloud, "per-se-cu-test—per-se-cu-test—per-se-cu-test—per-se-cu-test!" And as I peeped into the brush-pile, again the brown thrush, building within, said, "thou—thou—thou!"

Through all the years since I had thought myself changed, and craved no greater glory than to be accounted the chief of their apostles. But now I was stained once more with the old guilt, and once more I could hear the birds in my yard singing that old, old chorus against man's inhumanity.

Towards the middle of the afternoon I went away across the country—by any direction; I cared not what. On my way back I passed through a large rear lot belonging to my neighbors, and adjoining my own, in which is my stable. There has lately been imported into this part of Kentucky from England the much-prized breed of the beautiful white Berkshire. As I crossed the lot, near the milk-trough, ash-heap, and parings of fruit and vegetables thrown from my neighbor's kitchen, I saw a litter of these pigs having their awkward sport over some strange red plaything, which one after another of them would shake with all its might, root and tear at, or tread into greater shapelessness. It was all there was left of him.

I entered my long yard. If I could have been spared the sight of that! The sun was setting. Around me was the last peace and beauty of the world. Through a narrow avenue of trees I could see my house, and on its clustering vines fell the angry red of the sun darting across the cool green fields.

The last hour of light touches the birds as it touches us. When they sing in the morning, it is with the happiness of the earth; but as the shadows fall strangely about them, and the helplessness of the night comes on, their voices seem to be lifted up like the loftiest poetry of the human spirit, with sympathy for realities and mysteries past all understanding.

A great choir was hymning now. On the tops of the sweet old honeysuckles the catbirds; robins in the low boughs of maples; on the high limb of the elm the silvery-throated lark, who had stopped as he passed from meadow to meadow; on a fence rail of the distant wheat-field the quail—and many another. I walked to and fro, receiving the voice of each as a spear hurled at my body. The sun sank. The shadows rushed on and deepened. Suddenly, as I turned once more in my path, I caught sight of the figure of Georgiana moving straight towards me from the direction of the garden. She was bareheaded, dressed in white; and she advanced over the smooth lawn, through evergreens and shrubs, with a gentle grace and dignity of movement such as I had never beheld. I kept my weary pace, and when she came up I did not lift my eyes.

"Adam!" she said, with gentle reproach. I stood still then, but with my face turned away.

"Forgive me!" All girlishness was gone out of her voice. It was the woman at last.

I turned my face farther from her, and we stood in silence.

"I have suffered enough, Adam," she pleaded.

I answered quietly, doggedly, for there was nothing left in me to appeal to:

"I am glad we can part kindly. . . . Neither of us may care much for the kindness now, but we will not be sorry hereafter. . . . The quarrels, the mistakes, the right and the wrong of our lives, the misunderstandings—they are so strange, so pitiful, so full of pain, and come so soon to nothing." And I lifted my hat, and took the path towards my house.

There was a point ahead where it divided, the other branch leading towards the little private gate through which Georgiana had come. Just before reaching the porch I looked that way, with the idea that I should see Georgiana's white figure moving across the lawn; but I discovered that she was following me. Mounting my door-steps, I turned. She had paused on the threshold. I waited. At length she said, in a voice low and sorrowful:

"And you are not going to forgive me, Adam?"

"I do forgive you!" The silence fell and lasted. I no longer saw her face. At last her despairing voice barely reached me again:

"And—is—that—all?"

I had no answer to make, and sternly waited for her to go.

A moment longer she lingered, then turned slowly away; and I watched her figure growing fainter and fainter till it was lost. I sprang after her; my voice rang out hollow, and broke with terror and pain and longing:

"Georgiana! Georgiana!"

"Oh, Adam, Adam!" I heard her cry, with low, piercing tenderness, as she ran back to me through the darkness.

When we separated we lighted fresh candles and set them in our windows, to burn a pure pathway of flame across the intervening void. Henceforth we are like poor little foolish children, so sick and lonesome in the night without one another. Happy, happy night to come when one short candle will do for us both!

. . . Ah, but the long, long silence of the trees! . . .

The Codes Of Hammurabi And Moses
W. W. Davies

QTY

The discovery of the Hammurabi Code is one of the greatest achievements of archaeology, and is of paramount interest, not only to the student of the Bible, but also to all those interested in ancient history...

Religion   **ISBN:** *1-59462-338-4*   **Pages:132**
MSRP $12.95

The Theory of Moral Sentiments
Adam Smith

QTY

This work from 1749. contains original theories of conscience amd moral judgment and it is the foundation for systemof morals.

Philosophy **ISBN:** *1-59462-777-0*   **Pages:536**
MSRP $19.95

Jessica's First Prayer
Hesba Stretton

QTY

In a screened and secluded corner of one of the many railway-bridges which span the streets of London there could be seen a few years ago, from five o'clock every morning until half past eight, a tidily set-out coffee-stall, consisting of a trestle and board, upon which stood two large tin cans, with a small fire of charcoal burning under each so as to keep the coffee boiling during the early hours of the morning when the work-people were thronging into the city on their way to their daily toil...

Pages:84

Childrens   **ISBN:** *1-59462-373-2*   *MSRP $9.95*

My Life and Work
Henry Ford

QTY

Henry Ford revolutionized the world with his implementation of mass production for the Model T automobile. Gain valuable business insight into his life and work with his own auto-biography... "We have only started on our development of our country we have not as yet, with all our talk of wonderful progress, done more than scratch the surface. The progress has been wonderful enough but..."

Pages:300

Biographies/   **ISBN:** *1-59462-198-5*   *MSRP $21.95*

The Art of Cross-Examination
Francis Wellman

QTY

I presume it is the experience of every author, after his first book is published upon an important subject, to be almost overwhelmed with a wealth of ideas and illustrations which could readily have been included in his book, and which to his own mind, at least, seem to make a second edition inevitable. Such certainly was the case with me; and when the first edition had reached its sixth impression in five months, I rejoiced to learn that it seemed to my publishers that the book had met with a sufficiently favorable reception to justify a second and considerably enlarged edition. ..

Pages:412

Reference   ISBN: *1-59462-647-2*   *MSRP $19.95*

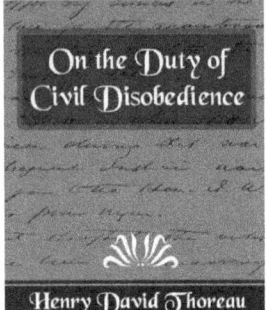

On the Duty of Civil Disobedience
Henry David Thoreau

QTY

Thoreau wrote his famous essay, On the Duty of Civil Disobedience, as a protest against an unjust but popular war and the immoral but popular institution of slave-owning. He did more than write—he declined to pay his taxes, and was hauled off to gaol in consequence. Who can say how much this refusal of his hastened the end of the war and of slavery ?

Law   ISBN: *1-59462-747-9*

Pages:48
MSRP $7.45

Dream Psychology Psychoanalysis for Beginners
Sigmund Freud

QTY

Sigmund Freud, born Sigismund Schlomo Freud (May 6, 1856 - September 23, 1939), was a Jewish-Austrian neurologist and psychiatrist who co-founded the psychoanalytic school of psychology. Freud is best known for his theories of the unconscious mind, especially involving the mechanism of repression; his redefinition of sexual desire as mobile and directed towards a wide variety of objects; and his therapeutic techniques, especially his understanding of transference in the therapeutic relationship and the presumed value of dreams as sources of insight into unconscious desires.

Pages:196

Psychology   ISBN: *1-59462-905-6*   *MSRP $15.45*

The Miracle of Right Thought
Orison Swett Marden

QTY

Believe with all of your heart that you will do what you were made to do. When the mind has once formed the habit of holding cheerful, happy, prosperous pictures, it will not be easy to form the opposite habit. It does not matter how improbable or how far away this realization may see, or how dark the prospects may be, if we visualize them as best we can, as vividly as possible, hold tenaciously to them and vigorously struggle to attain them, they will gradually become actualized, realized in the life. But a desire, a longing without endeavor, a yearning abandoned or held indifferently will vanish without realization.

Pages:360

Self Help   ISBN: *1-59462-644-8*   *MSRP $25.45*

QTY

The Rosicrucian Cosmo-Conception Mystic Christianity by *Max Heindel*   ISBN: *1-59462-188-8*   **$38.95**
The Rosicrucian Cosmo-conception is not dogmatic, neither does it appeal to any other authority than the reason of the student. It is: not controversial, but is: sent forth in the, hope that it may help to clear...   New Age/Religion Pages 646

Abandonment To Divine Providence by *Jean-Pierre de Caussade*   ISBN: *1-59462-228-0*   **$25.95**
"The Rev. Jean Pierre de Caussade was one of the most remarkable spiritual writers of the Society of Jesus in France in the 18th Century. His death took place at Toulouse in 1751. His works have gone through many editions and have been republished...   Inspirational/Religion Pages 400

Mental Chemistry by *Charles Haanel*   ISBN: *1-59462-192-6*   **$23.95**
Mental Chemistry allows the change of material conditions by combining and appropriately utilizing the power of the mind. Much like applied chemistry creates something new and unique out of careful combinations of chemicals the mastery of mental chemistry...   New Age Pages 354

The Letters of Robert Browning and Elizabeth Barret Barrett 1845-1846 vol II   ISBN: *1-59462-193-4*   **$35.95**
by *Robert Browning* and *Elizabeth Barrett*   Biographies Pages 596

Gleanings In Genesis (volume I) by *Arthur W. Pink*   ISBN: *1-59462-130-6*   **$27.45**
Appropriately has Genesis been termed "the seed plot of the Bible" for in it we have, in germ form, almost all of the great doctrines which are afterwards fully developed in the books of Scripture which follow...   Religion/Inspirational Pages 420

The Master Key by *L. W. de Laurence*   ISBN: *1-59462-001-6*   **$30.95**
In no branch of human knowledge has there been a more lively increase of the spirit of research during the past few years than in the study of Psychology, Concentration and Mental Discipline. The requests for authentic lessons in Thought Control, Mental Discipline and...   New Age/Business Pages 422

The Lesser Key Of Solomon Goetia by *L. W. de Laurence*   ISBN: *1-59462-092-X*   **$9.95**
This translation of the first book of the "Lernegton" which is now for the first time made accessible to students of Talismanic Magic was done, after careful collation and edition, from numerous Ancient Manuscripts in Hebrew, Latin, and French...   New Age/Occult Pages 92

Rubaiyat Of Omar Khayyam by *Edward Fitzgerald*   ISBN:*1-59462-332-5*   **$13.95**
Edward Fitzgerald, whom the world has already learned, in spite of his own efforts to remain within the shadow of anonymity, to look upon as one of the rarest poets of the century, was born at Bredfield, in Suffolk, on the 31st of March, 1809. He was the third son of John Purcell...   Music Pages 172

Ancient Law by *Henry Maine*   ISBN: *1-59462-128-4*   **$29.95**
The chief object of the following pages is to indicate some of the earliest ideas of mankind, as they are reflected in Ancient Law, and to point out the relation of those ideas to modern thought.   Religion/History Pages 452

Far-Away Stories by *William J. Locke*   ISBN: *1-59462-129-2*   **$19.45**
"Good wine needs no bush, but a collection of mixed vintages does. And this book is just such a collection. Some of the stories I do not want to remain buried for ever in the museum files of dead magazine-numbers an author's not unpardonable vanity..."   Fiction Pages 272

Life of David Crockett by *David Crockett*   ISBN: *1-59462-250-7*   **$27.45**
"Colonel David Crockett was one of the most remarkable men of the times in which he lived. Born in humble life, but gifted with a strong will, an indomitable courage, and unremitting perseverance...   Biographies/New Age Pages 424

Lip-Reading by *Edward Nitchie*   ISBN: *1-59462-206-X*   **$25.95**
Edward B. Nitchie, founder of the New York School for the Hard of Hearing, now the Nitchie School of Lip-Reading, Inc, wrote "LIP-READING Principles and Practice". The development and perfecting of this meritorious work on lip-reading was an undertaking...   How-to Pages 400

A Handbook of Suggestive Therapeutics, Applied Hypnotism, Psychic Science   ISBN: *1-59462-214-0*   **$24.95**
by *Henry Munro*   Health/New Age/Health/Self-help Pages 376

A Doll's House: and Two Other Plays by *Henrik Ibsen*   ISBN: *1-59462-112-8*   **$19.95**
Henrik Ibsen created this classic when in revolutionary 1848 Rome. Introducing some striking concepts in playwriting for the realist genre, this play has been studied the world over.   Fiction/Classics/Plays 308

The Light of Asia by *sir Edwin Arnold*   ISBN: *1-59462-204-3*   **$13.95**
In this poetic masterpiece, Edwin Arnold describes the life and teachings of Buddha. The man who was to become known as Buddha to the world was born as Prince Gautama of India but he rejected the worldly riches and abandoned the reigns of power when...   Religion/History/Biographies Pages 170

The Complete Works of Guy de Maupassant by *Guy de Maupassant*   ISBN: *1-59462-157-8*   **$16.95**
"For days and days, nights and nights, I had dreamed of that first kiss which was to consecrate our engagement, and I knew not on what spot I should put my lips..."   Fiction/Classics Pages 240

The Art of Cross-Examination by *Francis L. Wellman*   ISBN: *1-59462-309-0*   **$26.95**
Written by a renowned trial lawyer, Wellman imparts his experience and uses case studies to explain how to use psychology to extract desired information through questioning.   How-to/Science/Reference Pages 408

Answered or Unanswered? by *Louisa Vaughan*   ISBN: *1-59462-248-5*   **$10.95**
Miracles of Faith in China   Religion Pages 112

The Edinburgh Lectures on Mental Science (1909) by *Thomas*   ISBN: *1-59462-008-3*   **$11.95**
This book contains the substance of a course of lectures recently given by the writer in the Queen Street Hall, Edinburgh. Its purpose is to indicate the Natural Principles governing the relation between Mental Action and Material Conditions...   New Age/Psychology Pages 148

Ayesha by *H. Rider Haggard*   ISBN: *1-59462-301-5*   **$24.95**
Verily and indeed it is the unexpected that happens! Probably if there was one person upon the earth from whom the Editor of this, and of a certain previous history, did not expect to hear again...   Classics Pages 380

Ayala's Angel by *Anthony Trollope*   ISBN: *1-59462-352-X*   **$29.95**
The two girls were both pretty, but Lucy who was twenty-one who supposed to be simple and comparatively unattractive, whereas Ayala was credited, as her Bombwhat romantic name might show, with poetic charm and a taste for romance. Ayala when her father died was nineteen...   Fiction Pages 484

The American Commonwealth by *James Bryce*   ISBN: *1-59462-286-8*   **$34.45**
An interpretation of American democratic political theory. It examines political mechanics and society from the perspective of Scotsman James Bryce   Politics Pages 572

Stories of the Pilgrims by *Margaret P. Pumphrey*   ISBN: *1-59462-116-0*   **$17.95**
This book explores pilgrims religious oppression in England as well as their escape to Holland and eventual crossing to America on the Mayflower, and their early days in New England...   History Pages 268

QTY

The Fasting Cure *by Sinclair Upton* ISBN: *1-59462-222-1* **$13.95**
*In the Cosmopolitan Magazine for May, 1910, and in the Contemporary Review (London) for April, 1910, I published an article dealing with my experi-
ences in fasting. I have written a great many magazine articles, but never one which attracted so much attention...* New Age/Self Help/Health Pages 164

Hebrew Astrology *by Sepharial* ISBN: *1-59462-308-2* **$13.45**
*In these days of advanced thinking it is a matter of common observation that we have left many of the old landmarks behind and that we are now pressing
forward to greater heights and to a wider horizon than that which represented the mind-content of our progenitors...* Astrology Pages 144

Thought Vibration or The Law of Attraction in the Thought World ISBN: *1-59462-127-6* **$12.95**
by William Walker Atkinson Psychology/Religion Pages 144

Optimism *by Helen Keller* ISBN: *1-59462-108-X* **$15.95**
*Helen Keller was blind, deaf, and mute since 19 months old, yet famously learned how to overcome these handicaps, communicate with the world, and
spread her lectures promoting optimism. An inspiring read for everyone...* Biographies/Inspirational Pages 84

Sara Crewe *by Frances Burnett* ISBN: *1-59462-360-0* **$9.45**
*In the first place, Miss Minchin lived in London. Her home was a large, dull, tall one, in a large, dull square, where all the houses were alike, and all the
sparrows were alike, and where all the door-knockers made the same heavy sound...* Childrens/Classic Pages 88

The Autobiography of Benjamin Franklin *by Benjamin Franklin* ISBN: *1-59462-135-7* **$24.95**
*The Autobiography of Benjamin Franklin has probably been more extensively read than any other American historical work, and no other book of its kind
has had such ups and downs of fortune. Franklin lived for many years in England, where he was agent...* Biographies/History Pages 332

Name	
Email	
Telephone	
Address	
City, State ZIP	

☐ **Credit Card**   ☐ **Check / Money Order**

Credit Card Number	
Expiration Date	
Signature	

*Please Mail to: Book Jungle
PO Box 2226
Champaign, IL 61825
or Fax to: 630-214-0564*

ORDERING INFORMATION

web*: www.bookjungle.com*
email*: sales@bookjungle.com*
fax*: 630-214-0564*
mail*: Book Jungle PO Box 2226 Champaign, IL 61825*
or PayPal *to sales@bookjungle.com*

Please contact us for bulk discounts

DIRECT-ORDER TERMS

**20% Discount if You Order
Two or More Books**
Free Domestic Shipping!
Accepted: Master Card, Visa,
Discover, American Express

www.ingramcontent.com/pod-product-compliance
Lightning Source LLC
Chambersburg PA
CBHW081201170626
46813CB00009B/3272